TOPZ SECRET STORIES

Dixons' Den

Alexa Tewkesbury

CWR

Published 2012 by CWR, Waverley Abbey House, Waverley Lane, Farnham, Surrey GU9 8EP, UK. Registered Charity No. 294387. Registered Limited Company No. 1990308.

See back of book for list of National Distributors.
All Scriptures quoted from the International Children's Bible, New Century Version (Anglicised Edition) copyright © 1991 by Nelson Word Ltd, Milton Keynes, England. Used by permission.

Concept development, editing, design and production by CWR
Illustrations: Mike Henson at CWR
Printed in Finland by Bookwell
ISBN: 978-1-85345-690-9

Hey!
I'm Kevin – I'm in the Dixons Gang.

You might have heard of us. There's me and my mates, Rick and Clyde, and we all live on the Dixons Estate, in Holly Hill.

There's not that much to do in Holly Hill so we like to hang out together. The best places are the shopping centre and the park – there's lots of room there to play football or ride a bike.

Sometimes we run into the Topz Gang. 'Topzies' we call them just cos it bugs them. They're really annoying – they always seem to be talking about God and I don't get it. Us Dixons, we're cool. But Topz, they're just a waste of space.

That's why I'm so glad we've got a new place to hang out now. If you're not a Dixon, stay away – it's ours, Dixons' Den. No one else goes there. No one else knows where it is.

That's what this story is all about ...

Hi! We're the Topz Gang –

Topz because we all live at the 'top' of something …
either in houses at the top of the hill, at the top of the
flats by the park, even sleeping in a top bunk counts!
We are all Christians, and we go to Holly Hill School.
We love Jesus, and try to work out our faith in God
in everything we do – at home, at school and with our
friends. That even means trying to show God's love to
the Dixons Gang who tend to be bullies, and can be a
real pain!

If you'd like to know more about us, visit our website
at **www.cwr.org.uk/topz** You can read all about us,
and how you can get to know and understand the Bible
more by reading our *Topz* notes, which are great fun,
and written every two months just for you!

One

The room was empty.

There was nothing left at all.

The last thing to go was Saf's chest of drawers.
It was her favourite piece of furniture in her bedroom;
wooden and chunky. Saf's dad had painted it bright
green with a daisy chain pattern curling its way across
the front of each drawer. None of her friends had
anything like it in their rooms. What Saf loved best was
that it had been her mum's chest of drawers when she
was a girl.

Now it stood in the back of the removal lorry parked
outside the front gate. Jammed in with everything else.
The beds, chairs, sofa, table, cooker, fridge, TV – not to
mention all the boxes and boxes of clothes and books
and toys and bits and pieces it felt as if they'd been
packing up for weeks. What was it Saf's mum used to
say when they'd overloaded the car for their camping
holidays? 'Everything but the kitchen sink …'

Saf sat on her bedroom floor under the window.
Exactly where the chest of drawers had stood five
minutes earlier. The room looked so big without
anything in it. Even the ceiling
seemed much further away.
And everything echoed. When a
removal man put his head round
the door, his voice rang around
the bare walls: 'Nothing left in
here, then?'

Saf didn't answer. It was obvious,
wasn't it?

'You excited about moving to your new place?'
the man went on, cheerfully.

She pressed her lips more tightly together and shook
her head.

'Sure you are,' smiled the man. 'Bet you'll love it once
you get settled in.'

But Saf knew she wouldn't love it. She'd known from
the moment her dad had announced they were leaving.
Holly Hill was miles away. Nearly three hours in the car.
It was a town, with row after row of houses and tall
blocks of flats. The tallest things Saf was used to living
near were the trees in the woods on the edge of her
village. There was even an apple tree in their garden.
Nothing like that was growing in the garden of their
new house. Not in Holly Hill.

It was all Auntie Becky's fault.

Auntie Becky was Saf's mum's older sister. 'Bex has
always been bossy,' Saf remembered her mum saying
with a smile more than once.

'Pete, if you find it too hard managing with the two
kids on your own, you can always move to Holly Hill to
be near us,' Auntie Becky had said to Saf's dad. 'Then
we can lend a hand. Anyway, we'd love it.'

That's what had started her dad thinking. That's
why he'd found a new job as a maths teacher at
the secondary school near Holly Hill. That's why this
summer, the holidays weren't about long, light days
and reading books and playing with friends. They were
about moving house.

That's why Saf was sitting in an empty bedroom.

'Why does Dad need help "managing" anyway?'
she had complained to her younger brother, Stephen.
'It's not as if we're naughty or anything. "Be good

for your dad", that's what Mum said, and we are. We help, don't we, Stevie? I even taught you to tie your shoelaces. Why do we have to go just because Auntie Becky says so?'

Stevie didn't seem to mind. 'My room's going to be bigger there, Saf,' he answered happily. 'And Daddy says I can have racing car wallpaper.'

He'll never understand, Saf thought.

But then Stevie was only six, so how could he?

As the rooms in the house were cleared, one by one, the tinny roar of the old hoover filled the air. 'Time to get a new one of these, too,' Pete remarked as he did the last bits of cleaning as quickly as he could.

'Lots of dust, Daddy!' Saf heard Stevie squeal excitedly. 'Saf, come and see! There's so much dust!'

Pete clattered the hoover down by her bedroom door. 'Do the carpet in here, would you, please, Saf?' he said. Then, without waiting for an answer, he shot off to see what else still needed doing. They were leaving. All he wanted now was to get out of there as soon as possible.

Saf didn't hoover. Instead, she slipped downstairs, through the kitchen, and out of the back door into the garden. The grass was newly cut. Her dad had whisked over it with the lawnmower yesterday evening. She sat down under the apple tree, her back against the trunk that leaned just slightly towards the hedge. The branches over her head were full of baby apples. Small, green; almost rock hard. Saf cast her eyes over them. She'd seen them from their very beginning. The pink-tipped buds had started to appear in early April. By the first days of May, they were fully open, and the tree was covered in frothy blossom.

'Why doesn't the blossom smell of apples?' Stevie had asked. He and Saf had watched the flowers come and go. But their mum hadn't seen any of it this year. Not the blossom; not the early apples. And now Saf wouldn't even get to taste one ripe apple from this year's crop.

Suddenly, she felt tears stinging in her eyes. Was she crying? She hadn't cried for weeks. Months.

Four months and three days.

That last time, she'd cried so much, she thought her tears would run out completely.

'Saf!' Pete's voice reached her through her open bedroom window. He sounded annoyed. 'Saf, where are you? I asked you to hoover in here.'

'I'll do it, Daddy,' she heard Stevie offer, eagerly.

'Go on, then, just for a minute,' Pete answered. 'Saf, where have you got to now?'

Saf rubbed her fists into her eyes. 'Don't you cry,' she whispered to herself. 'Angry people don't cry.'

A moment later, her dad was standing beside her. 'Saffron, I could really do with your help this morning, you know.'

Saf didn't answer. She couldn't. She was still trying to swallow down the lump in her throat.

'Why must you be so difficult about this?' Pete went on. 'I'm only trying to do what's best for us. I know it all seems like a huge wrench at the moment, but you'll feel better once we've left here and got settled in. And you'll have your cousin practically on your doorstep. Auntie Becky says Rhianna can't wait till you're living there. Oh, come on, Saf,' and Pete gave her a nudge with his elbow. 'Give us a smile, eh?'

But Saf didn't smile. Just at that moment it felt as though she'd never be able to smile again.

'Daddy!' Stevie called from upstairs. 'Daddy, I can't get the hoover to switch on.'

Saf scrambled to her feet. 'Leave it, Stevie, I'll do it,' she shouted, brushing past her dad as she ran inside.

Hours later, after a long drive, a nibble on a few dry sandwiches and a lot of unloading, there the three of them were: in their new house.

Auntie Becky, Uncle Nick and Rhianna had dropped by with a tray of tea, blackcurrant squash and some chocolate biscuits but Saf didn't feel much like talking.

'She hasn't said a word all the way here,' she heard her dad sigh to Auntie Becky and Uncle Nick at the front door as they were leaving.

'Don't worry about it, Pete,' Auntie Becky replied. 'She'll come round. You'll sort her out, won't you, Rhianna?'

Finally left alone, Saf sat in her new bedroom and glanced about her at the muddle of furniture and boxes. The removal men had dumped everything in a haphazard way. Her bed was pushed up against one wall. The chest of drawers couldn't go under the window like in her old room, because there was a radiator already there. In fact, because of the built-in wardrobe, the only real space for it was by the door where the men had put it. It didn't look the same. In her old room, Saf liked the way her long curtains hung down either side of it. Here, the chest hardly looked like hers at all.

Slowly, she opened a cardboard packing case full of her clothes. She couldn't hang anything up yet. She didn't know where the hangers were. Another box held her books, and the third one had some board games and the cuddly toys she'd had since she was little. Her dad had hoped she would give some of them away to a charity shop. After all, she was bigger now and the less they had

to pack up and move the better. But Saf had refused.
'I'm not leaving anything else behind!'
she'd shouted. 'You can't make me!'

Right on the top of the box was Rachel, a cream-coloured, floppy-eared toy rabbit. Saf's mum had given it to her for being brave on her first ever day at school. Saf lifted her out. Even the rabbit looked sad somehow, all wrong in this new bedroom; like everything else.

'I know, Rachel,' Saf whispered. 'I'm sad, too.'

Her dad's head appeared round the door. 'Getting on all right in here?'

She barely nodded.

'Well, I've found the bedding at least,' he went on. He dropped a bundle of sheets, duvet and a pillow on Saf's mattress. 'I'm just going to get the beds made up, then we're popping over to Auntie Becky's for supper. I told her we could get pizza but she says she's already got something. I'll do your bed first, shall I?'

'No, I'll do it,' Saf answered.

'I don't mind,' smiled Pete.

Saf shook her head. 'It's fine, I want to.'

Pete was pleased. Saf wanted to help, that must be

a good sign, he thought. As he went off to make up Stevie's bed, he wondered if Auntie Becky was right and Saf was coming round to the move already.

Saf wasn't.

She sat down on the bare mattress then swung her feet up, kicking the bedding onto the floor and stretching out on her back. How weird, she thought, that the last time she'd lain on her bed, it had been in her old room. Very early that same day. Now it seemed a million hours away. A million miles away.

But then everything did. Only a year ago, Saf could never have imagined the huge changes that lay ahead for her whole family. None of them could.

Her mum had got ill; seriously ill. Then four months and three days ago, she had died.

'I just want to help you feel better, Mum,' Saf had said to her, snuggled up beside her on the sofa one day. 'What can I do?'

'You can be good for your dad, Saffy,' her mum had smiled. 'You and Stevie. And you can pray for me, sweetheart. I'd like that.'

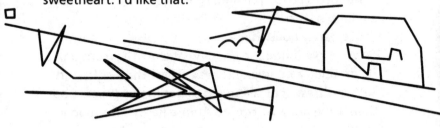

Two

'I could be the donkey, too!' Benny suggested enthusiastically. 'There has to be a donkey to carry the injured man to the inn to be looked after. Jesus says so at the end of the story. So I could be the donkey *and* a robber.'

The Topz Gang, and Rhianna and Eddie from Sunday Club, were sitting in Paul's garden. They were working on the next LIFE STARTS HERE performance, their very own church drama group. Sarah had thought up the name. So far they'd acted out several of the stories Jesus told in the Bible, including the parable of the wise and foolish builders. That one had been their first ever production.

This time, they'd decided on the good Samaritan, the story of a man attacked by robbers. As he lay bleeding in the road, he was ignored by two priests, who saw him but simply hurried on past. It was a man from Samaria who finally rescued him. He showed God's love by being a friend to someone who needed help.

'I'd be a brilliant donkey!' Benny insisted. 'I know how donkeys move.'

'What, on four legs, you mean?' Paul replied.

'Well, of course on four legs,' Benny said, 'but it's not just about shuffling around – there's a real knack to it, you know. You have to know how to do things like that when you're an actor.'

'The trouble is,' added Josie doubtfully, 'if Eddie's the other robber then he should get the chance to be a donkey, too. But there's only one donkey in the story.'

'I don't mind being just a robber,' Eddie answered.

Benny leapt to his feet excitedly. 'Got it! We can *both* be the donkey. We can get hold of one of those donkey suits they wear in pantomimes! Then one of us can be the front half and one of us the back.'

'Yeah, but this isn't a pantomime, is it, Benny?' said Danny. 'It's meant to be serious. If you both come in dressed in a donkey suit, people will just laugh.'

'Why?' Benny frowned. 'It's all acting. No one's going to laugh when you come in dressed as a man from Samaria, are they?'

There was silence.

'Anyone for ice cream?' asked Paul.

'Great! What flavour is it?' asked Benny. He was easily distracted by food.

Rhianna stood up, slipping on her cardigan. 'Actually, sorry, Paul, but I should probably go.'

'We should go, too, Sarah,' agreed Josie. 'Mum'll be waiting for us to help her sort out the stuff for the car boot sale.'

'Yeah, bye guys,' said Sarah as the three of them headed out of the back gate. 'Good luck sorting the donkey thing!'

Josie glanced at Rhianna as they walked. 'Is everything all right? You're really quiet today.'

'Just thinking about Saf, that's all,' Rhianna answered. 'I'm worried about her.'

Sarah and Josie had met Saf. Just once at church last Sunday. It was obvious she didn't want to be there. Rhianna had invited her, then her dad had pushed her into going.

'Come on,' Pete had said, 'we'll all go. Be good for you *and* Stevie. You can both start getting to know some of the other kids round here. Rhianna says quite a few of Sunday Club go to the primary school.'

Saf didn't care. She didn't want to meet Sunday Club, or anyone else in Holly Hill for that matter. Hadn't she been pushed around enough being taken away from her home? She certainly wasn't going to be pushed into friendships she didn't want. Anyway, she already had friends at her old school. Her proper school. The one in the village her dad had forced her to leave. Not that she'd had much to do with them in the months since her mum had died. She hadn't had much to do with anyone.

Sarah and Josie knew all about Saf before she turned up at church. Rhianna was so excited to have her cousins moving in just a few streets away that she'd been telling everyone.

'It'll be like having a twin sister and little brother!' she gabbled to Topz when she first heard the news. 'It's so sad about their mum – my Auntie Teri was lovely – but at least they're coming to live here now. We can help make it all better.'

But, from the moment Saf had moved in, it was obvious that 'making it all better' wasn't going to be easy. Saf and Rhianna had got on well enough when they'd met up for occasional family days, but now Saf just wasn't talking. Not to anyone and Rhianna didn't know what to do. Last Sunday had been really awkward. Rhianna had done her best to introduce Saf at Sunday Club, and Topz had made a huge effort to be welcoming. But she'd hardly even looked at anyone let alone talked to them. Apart, that is, from one blunt response.

'It must be really hard moving somewhere new after everything that's happened,' Sarah had said kindly.

'You'll have to come and hang around with us. We have loads of laughs. And Rhianna's in our drama group. You can join, too, if you like. We're going to start practising for a new performance this week.'

'Well,' interrupted Josie, 'when Sarah says we're going to start practising, we've actually got to write the script first.'

'You could help us do that, Saf!' Sarah cried, full of excitement at the possibilities there were in having a new friend.

'No, thanks,' Saf answered quietly. 'I don't like drama.'

And that was it. That was all she'd said all Sunday morning.

As the girls reached Rhianna's house after their good Samaritan meeting, Josie said, 'Everything'll be all right. Saf'll like it here in the end, she's sure to. I mean, she hasn't even been here a week yet, has she?'

'A week tomorrow,' said Rhianna quietly.

'There you are, then. It would take me much longer than a week to get used to somewhere new.'

'And me,' added Sarah. 'Especially if I had to leave Topz. And as for losing your mum … Don't know how anyone ever gets used to that.'

'No,' said Rhianna flatly. 'It's just … I was *so* excited she was going to be living here. I really thought it would be like having a sister. But, it hasn't turned out like that at all.'

'We need to pray for her,' Josie replied. 'I mean, really, *really* pray for her. We need to make her top of the Topz prayer list. God makes things better. Not straight away maybe, but in the end He always makes things better. It's just up to us to ask Him to.'

Rhianna nodded. 'Yeah, you're right. God can make things better. **I'll pray, too.'**

A week after their move, Saf's new home was just about unpacked. They'd found a place for most things. Anything Pete wasn't sure what to do with was left boxed up and stowed away in the loft. Some of it had come straight from the loft in their old house. Saf's mum used to say, 'You never know when it might come in useful.' She wasn't good at clearing out. 'Don't like getting rid of things, don't like change,' she'd laugh.

And Saf was just like her. She hated this new life. It was unrecognisable from the way things used to be. Their 'comfortably complete family of four', as her mum called them, was all broken up. However cheerful her dad wanted to sound, however much he tried to get Saf into doing this, that and the other, that's just the way it was now. As far as Saf was concerned, he'd dragged them away from their home to this miserable place and she'd never get used to it. Their family was in pieces without her mum there to hold them together.

And it hurt. It really hurt.

There was one space, though, that Saf found she quite liked in this place she didn't like at all. The park. She wasn't interested in the swings or the roundabout or the climbing frame. She didn't want to play. Saf liked the park because it was big and open, with grass and trees and even a large pond. It was a patch of countryside in amongst the tall buildings and noisy roads.

Not that Holly Hill was a bad town. It just wasn't what she was used to. The park, on the other hand, was different. And it was only a short walk from their house. Rhianna had told her she went there all the time, although Saf hadn't seen her down there yet – which she didn't mind a bit.

'Off to the park *again?*' asked Pete when he saw her in the kitchen, putting on her cycling helmet.

Saf shrugged. 'Nowhere else to go, is there?'

'Why don't you call for Rhianna on your way? Be nice if you went together.'

'No.' She shook her head. 'I'd rather go on my own.'

Pete sighed. Not out loud, but Saf could hear it in his voice as he said what he always did. 'Well, you take care on your bike. Promise me you'll only push it along the road. Don't start riding it till you get there.'

'I know, Dad, I'll be safe,' she said, opening the back door and heading for the shed. It was only small. With all the gardening bits and pieces rammed in there, together with Stevie's bike, Saf's bike only just fitted. Every time she went to get it out, it got hooked up on Stevie's stabilisers.

It was early, not quite 9 o'clock in the morning. The park should still be fairly quiet. Even in the short time Saf had been living in Holly Hill, she'd noticed that the play areas didn't start to fill up with other children and mums and dads and babies till later. There would be people walking to work, of course, but she didn't mind that. They were just passing through. It was when the little groups started to arrive to play that she didn't like it so much. She somehow felt as though she was being watched: *Why is that girl out here on her own? Hasn't she got any friends? Where's her family?*

Saf climbed onto her bike at the park gates. As she started to pedal along her usual route on the path, she was disappointed to see a few boys in the distance. They were playing football on the grass, well away from her, but it still felt like an intrusion. When she drew level with them, she thought she recognised them from Sunday Club. Some of the boys from that Topz Gang. She didn't want to stare, though, in case they saw her looking.

Leaving them behind, she rounded the bend in the path where it ran along beside the skateboard area. She was pushing down harder on the pedals to speed up, when a sudden jolt almost knocked her sideways.

'Not again,' she moaned. The chain had come off. It seemed to happen nearly every time she went out at the moment. 'Stupid bike.'

As Saf leant the bike against the railings beside her and bent down to fix it, a shadow fell across her.

Three shadows.

She squinted upwards. The sun was full in her eyes and at first she could only make out the three boys' outlines. They were bunched in around her.

She must have been right about the footballers, Saf thought. Topz – and they'd recognised her, too.

But it wasn't Topz. As Saf slowly made out the faces staring down at her, she realised she'd never seen them before. There was nothing friendly about them, either.

Just the opposite.

This was Dixons.

Three

Rick, Kevin and Clyde lived on the Dixons Estate. Just like Topz, they hung around with each other as much as they could. Just like Topz, they enjoyed messing about and having a laugh. They'd think up silly games and dare each other to do silly things. Just like Topz, the Dixons Gang were the best of friends.

Unlike Topz, though, Dixons were mean.

They were well known for it. Other kids kept out of their way.

Especially Topz.

Dixons hated them.

'Haven't seen you here before,' muttered Clyde. His red hair was sticking up at the front. It must have had some sort of gel in it. Either that or it badly needed washing, Saf thought.

Oddly, she didn't feel worried by the three boys clustered round her; just annoyed that she'd come to the park early to be by herself, and now she wasn't. She shrugged at them (she did a lot of shrugging these days) and turned her attention back to the chain on her bike.

Kevin nudged the front wheel with the toe of his trainer. 'What's up with that?' he wanted to know.

Saf shot him a glance. 'The chain's come off,' she grunted. 'What does it look like?'

'Looks like it's a rubbish bike,' sneered Rick. He blinked down at her through his over-long fringe.

Saf gave the chain a sharp tweak and it slipped back into place. 'Actually it's a really good bike,' she retorted, her chin jutting out crossly. 'Which is more than I can say for your haircut.'

Kevin couldn't help sniggering, but Rick's eyes seemed to go a shade darker. He took a step nearer Saf and closed his fists around the bike's handlebars. But whatever he was going to do was interrupted by another voice.

'All right, Saf?'

Benny and the three other Topz boys Saf had seen playing football were standing just behind them. They'd spotted her at the same time as she'd spotted them. But they'd caught sight of Dixons before her.

'Need any help with your bike?' Dave offered.

Saf stood up. 'Why is everyone so interested in my bike?' she frowned. 'Anyway, it's fine, I fixed it.'

'Well, if you ever do, Dave's good with bikes,' Paul added, nervously. He didn't feel comfortable this close to Dixons, even with his friends round him. 'He knows everything there is to know about bikes, Dave does. When he's older he wants to run a bike shop ...'

'Yeah, thanks, Paul,' Dave interrupted, 'but I don't think Saf needs to know about that right now.'

'No, probably not. Sorry,' Paul mumbled.

Danny gave Saf a smile. 'Don't know if you remember but we met you at Sunday Club last weekend.'

'Oh, no!' Clyde groaned. 'Just what Holly Hill needs – more Topz!'

Saf looked at him angrily. Who did these kids think they were? And as for the Topz Gang, what were they doing, barging over here like that? It wasn't as if she needed rescuing. Living in this place was getting worse and worse.

'I'm not Topz!' she snapped. 'I'm not anything. And I certainly don't belong in Holly Horrible Hill!'

She grabbed the bike's handlebars and yanked them away from Rick. He was so surprised, he let them go easily. Moments later, she'd shoved her way through the little crowd of boys and was pedalling furiously out of the park.

'Aw! I don't think she likes you,' said Kevin snidely, staring nastily at Benny, Danny, Paul and Dave. 'Being so *nicey-nice* hasn't worked on her, has it?'

Then Dixons sloped away.

Later, Dave rang Josie, and the two of them went to see Sarah and John.

'We're already praying for Saf,' Sarah said. 'If she doesn't want to be friends with us, I don't know what else we can do.' She was still feeling niggled that Saf had said she didn't like drama.

'Does she believe in God?' Dave asked.

'Rhianna doesn't know,' replied Josie. 'She says her mum did. Saf's mum's the one who gave Rhianna her Bible.'

'She really needs to know that He's there,' Dave went on. 'Things must be so hard for her.'

Sarah chewed her lip thoughtfully. 'I wonder if her dad realises how much she doesn't want to be here,' she said.

'Who knows?' Dave shook his head, then reached into his pocket and pulled out a piece of paper. 'I read this Bible verse this morning,' he went on, and read aloud the words he'd scribbled down: '"Saying the right word at the right time is so pleasing!" (Proverbs 15:23). Maybe that's what we could pray for Saf – that when we talk to her, we know what to say.'

'That's a great idea, Dave,' smiled Josie. 'That's how we should pray.'

'Yeah,' Sarah nodded. 'We should start straight away, too. And we should make sure we look out for Saf. She just seems so … angry.'

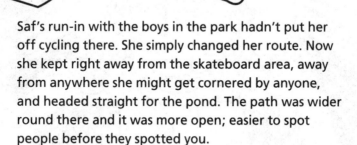

Saf's run-in with the boys in the park hadn't put her off cycling there. She simply changed her route. Now she kept right away from the skateboard area, away from anywhere she might get cornered by anyone, and headed straight for the pond. The path was wider round there and it was more open; easier to spot people before they spotted you.

Or so Saf thought.

When she found herself face to face with Kevin again, she wasn't expecting it at all but it was almost as if he'd been watching out for her.

A football slammed into the side of her bike as she cycled along. It didn't hit the back wheel hard enough to knock her off, but it did unbalance her.

'Whoa! That was a kick and a half!' Kevin bragged.

Saf turned her head sharply to see the Dixons boy sauntering towards her. His hands were stuffed into his pockets. He was clearly very pleased with himself for having hit a moving target. She curled her lip at him scornfully and went to ride away, but Kevin was too quick. In an instant he was standing in front of her bike, holding the handlebars.

'Wait a minute, what's the hurry?' he said.

'Let go,' Saf muttered.

'Why? What are you going to do if I don't?'

Saf didn't even hesitate. 'I'll ride into you.'

Kevin still didn't move.

'I mean it, I'll ride into you,' Saf repeated. Her eyes were locked onto the boy in front of her. If she was scared, she certainly wasn't going to let him see.

He stared back at her for a moment, then, 'I'll let go if you tell me something,' he said.

'Tell you what?'

'What have you got against the Topz Gang?'

'Sorry?' That was the last question Saf was expecting. What did Topz have to do with anything?

'The Topz Gang,' Kevin said again. 'Why don't you like them?'

Saf shook her head. 'I don't even know them.'

'Well, they seem to know you.'

'No, they don't. They've seen me around a bit, that's all.'

'So why are they looking out for you?'

'What is this?' Saf could feel herself getting cross. 'They're just kids I met in church. My cousin knows them. They're nothing to do with me. What's it to you anyway?'

Kevin's mouth twisted into a sneer. 'It's just that I'm in the Dixons Gang, and Topz and Dixons? We don't mix. You're new round here. I want to know whose side you're on.'

'I'm not on anyone's side. I don't even want to *be* here. The only reason we moved in the first place is because my dad made us.' Saf tried to pull her bike handlebars free from Kevin's grasp, but he didn't budge. 'Just get out of my way,' she snapped. 'I want to go.'

Kevin gave a half smile. 'I like the way you brushed them off,' he said. 'Those Topzies think they rule the place. You made them look like idiots.'

With that, he dropped his hands and stepped to one side. But instead of riding off, Saf carried on looking at him. She was the one who was curious now.

'So what is it with Topz and Dixons?' she asked. 'Why do you hate each other?'

Kevin laughed. 'Topz don't hate us,' he scoffed. 'They reckon they don't hate anyone. They do all this talking to God stuff and being all goody-goody all the time. That's what they were trying on you.' He grinned. 'Didn't work, though, did it?'

Saf hesitated a moment, her gaze still fixed on the Dixons boy.

'I'm sure Topz are OK,' she said finally. 'My cousin seems to like them and she's OK, I suppose, so they must be.'

She watched as a frown creased itself between Kevin's eyebrows. When he wasn't smiling, he looked quite different; almost as angry as Saf felt.

She carried on. 'But that doesn't mean I want to be friends with them. Or my cousin any more, really. She's told them things about me but it's none of her business. It's my life and it's up to me to talk about it if I feel like it, not some busybody behind my back.'

'I hate busybodies,' Kevin nodded.

'Anyway, I reckon they all feel sorry for me now, and I can't stand that … Besides …'

Saf paused. For the first time since Kevin had stepped in front of her bike, she dropped her gaze.

'What?' he asked.

She didn't answer.

'*What?*'

'It's my dad,' she said quietly. 'He's changed everything. Forever. It's as if the past doesn't matter any more. It does, though. It matters so much. More than what's going on here. More than any of this.' Her eyes flicked around the park and beyond, coming to rest on the nearby blocks of flats. They pointed towards the sky like thick fingers. 'My dad's even trying to push me into being friends with kids I don't want to be friends with. Well, it's not going to happen. I've got a mind of my own. I can think for myself. But it's like …' She trailed off.

Kevin was watching her, still frowning. She was a bit weird, this girl, he thought. But at the same time he really wanted to know what she was going to say.

'Like what?'

Saf looked at him again. 'Like no one's listening to me,' she replied simply. 'Everyone's making choices for me, decisions about what's best for my life. But no one's actually listening to what *I* want. Especially not my dad.'

'So what *do* you want?' Kevin asked.

'What do you care?'

He shrugged. 'Only asking. You're the one going on about it.'

Saf smiled at that. Just a little. 'I suppose I am. What's your name anyway?'

'Why, what's yours?'

'Saf. Well, Saffron, but everyone calls me Saf.'

'Kevin.'

'Do you get called Kev?'

'Sometimes. Don't really care either way.'

There was a pause. Then, 'So, Kevin, what's *your* dad like?' Saf asked. 'Is he a control freak like mine?'

'Dunno,' was the response.

It was Saf's turn to frown. 'What do you mean you don't know?'

Kevin stuck his hands back into his pockets. 'I don't know, do I? ... **He died.'**

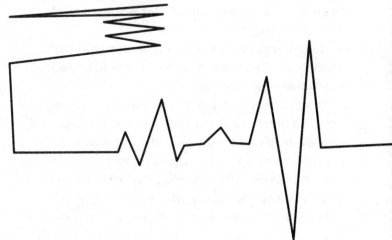

Four

Saf's eyes widened slightly. Kevin saw the surprise in her face.

'What?' he demanded.

'Your dad really died?' Saf said.

'Yeah,' he answered, a bit snappily. This girl got odder by the minute. 'That's why I said it.'

'When? When did he die?'

'Ages ago. I was about two or something. I've got a stepdad, but we don't really get on. When he's around at home I try and go out.' He smirked a little.

'Do you miss him?' Saf asked.

'What, you think I can remember that far back? I told you, I was only two. I've seen photos, that's about all. I mean, he sounded OK. My sister used to talk to me about him, but she's much older than me. She doesn't live here any more.'

Saf nodded thoughtfully.

'I know where he's buried,' Kevin went on. 'I used to go there. Mum never does. Not any more. Well, not since she married Mike anyway.'

Saf didn't say anything about her own mum. She wasn't sure she wanted this Dixons boy to know that much about her. Not yet.

It felt strange, though. There she was, standing in a park in a place she'd only lived in for a few days, and already she'd met someone who'd lost a parent, too. All right, so he was cocky and loud, and definitely a bully, but Kevin still knew what that felt like. He knew what it was to have someone missing.

If Saf did tell him about her mum – not that she

planned to, but just supposing she did – he was someone who might understand. Even if only a very little.

'Show me,' Saf said, suddenly.

Kevin looked at her as if she was mad. 'Show you? What, my dad's grave? Is there something wrong with you?'

'I'm just interested, that's all,' Saf replied. 'But if you don't want to – '

'No,' Kevin said quickly, 'no, it's not that. It's just … It's just not the sort of place anyone *normal* would want to go.'

Saf couldn't help smiling. 'I never said I was normal.'

'Just as well,' grinned Kevin, 'because you're weird!'

The town cemetery lay towards the edge of Holly Hill, on the far side of the shopping centre. It was quite a way from the park, but they walked quickly. Saf pushed her bike, and Kevin knew all the short cuts.

When they arrived, the tall, iron gates were standing open. They were quite rusty in places, and looked as if they might fall off their hinges if anyone tried to close them. As she and Kevin slipped inside, Saf gazed around at yet another place that was nothing like where she'd come from. The graveyard where her mum was buried was small and neat. The trees were kept trimmed and the hedges were cut. There were flowers, too, with brightly-coloured petals, growing in pots and clustered in vases. It was pretty, Saf thought. A pretty place to be.

This place wasn't pretty at all. It looked like a piece of rough ground that someone had one day decided to stick a fence around. Black-painted iron palings stood severely along the edges. Nearer to the gates it was tidier. The grass had been cut in perhaps the last couple of weeks. But the further away from the entrance Kevin led Saf, the scruffier the cemetery seemed to get.

There were odd bits of litter scattered amongst the headstones that sprawled across the lumpy ground. Some stones had a few flowers in front of them. They did their best to look cheerful as they straggled out of their containers. Others looked as if the graves they stood by were remembered or at least vaguely cared for. But others again were falling over or broken.

Mostly the headstones just looked sad. Bored somehow, Saf decided, as if, in spite of the names carved into their faces, they'd long ago forgotten why they were there.

They reached the side of the cemetery that was furthest from the town. Saf was so absorbed in what lay around her, that she didn't notice Kevin had stopped walking.

'Ow!' he yelped. 'Watch where you're going!'

She'd walked her bike right into him. 'Sorry. So where is it?'

Glancing around, Saf wasn't sure why Kevin had stopped. His dad's grave couldn't be here. There were no flowers at all. The grass didn't look as if it ever saw a lawnmower. And there were brambles; spiky, mean-looking tentacles that snaked their way around and through the iron palings.

'Kevin?'

Kevin nodded his head towards the patch of ground next to them.

Saf looked confused. 'But where's the headstone?'

'There isn't one. There's a marker, see?' Kevin crouched down and pulled at a thick tuft of grass.

A clump came away in his hand and there, sticking up behind where it had been growing, was a small wooden cross.

Saf laid her bike on the ground and bent down to get a closer look. There was a metal plate fixed to the cross. It was scuffed and dirty-looking, but she could still just about read the name engraved on it.

'Kevin Alan Cole. Is that him?' she asked quietly. 'Is that your dad?'

Kevin nodded.

'They named you after him.'

'Yeah,' he muttered. 'Just Kevin, though. Not Alan. I haven't got a middle name.'

'I have,' Saf replied. 'Guess what it is.'

'How should I know?'

'That's why you have to guess.'

'I don't know,' he groaned, but he was almost sure she wouldn't let it drop unless he guessed something. 'Mildred.'

'No!' Saf exclaimed. 'Do I look like a Mildred to you?'

'You look like a nutter to me.'

'Yeah? Well, do you know what?' she said, suddenly deadly serious. 'If being a nutter means I'd care that my dad was buried here, then I'm glad I look like a nutter.'

Kevin screwed up his face and peered at her, shaking his head. 'What are you on about now?'

'You. This!' Saf threw up her hands, staring miserably at Kevin Alan Cole's grave. 'Your dad's here and look at the mess. Why aren't you looking after it? You only live down the road. Don't you realise how lucky you are? You could come here all the time and make it nice. You could keep the grass cut. You could bring flowers. But what do you do?' she went on, jumping to her feet angrily.

'You spend your time picking on kids in the park! You should be ashamed of yourself!'

Kevin blinked in disbelief. No one spoke to him like that. Not even the kids who were bigger than he was. Certainly not *little* girls who were that bit younger and at least six inches shorter.

'You want to watch how you talk to me,' he snarled. His teeth were clenched tightly together. His eyes glittered. 'I only brought you here because you asked me to.'

'And I wish you hadn't!' Saf knew she should probably back off, but she was too upset. 'How could you let it get like this?' she blurted. 'Your poor dad! You've even got his name to remind you every day that he's here. How could you let it get in such a mess?'

'It's not my fault, is it?' he shouted, standing up and hurling down the clump of grass he still had in his hand. 'Mum stopped coming over here! It was up to her to keep it tidy, not me. I never even thought about it.'

'Well, you should have done!'

They stood still, staring at each other. Both breathless. Both boiling with anger.

Then suddenly Kevin turned and started to march furiously towards the cemetery gates.

'Where are you going?' yelled Saf.

'Home! You can find your own way back!'

Saf watched him striding away. Just for a moment. Then –

'At least you can visit here!' she screamed. 'Even if you don't think about your dad, at least you can visit if you want to. **I'll probably never see my mum's grave ever again!'**

Kevin stopped dead. What had Saf said? Her mum's *grave?*

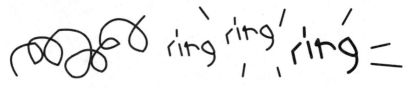

ring ring ring

Saf lay on her bed, gazing up at the ceiling. It was painted white like the ceiling in her old room. If she stared at it long enough and hard enough, until she'd blocked out everything else around her, she could almost imagine – *almost* – that she was back there.

Her dad had been cross when she'd got home earlier.

'You were gone for ages, Saf,' he said. 'I nearly came to the park looking for you. Why didn't you answer your phone?'

'We rang it loads,' added Stevie. 'I pressed the buttons.'

Saf had forgotten to switch it on. 'Sorry,' she answered. 'I lost track of time.'

'Well, it must have been a good cycle ride, that's all I can say,' Pete sighed. 'But another time, have your phone on, please.'

The cycle ride *was* good, but mostly what was good was that Saf had talked to Kevin. She'd eventually told him how her mum had died a few months ago; how she was buried in this pretty place that Saf couldn't get to because she was too far away. Saf wanted to be able to keep it tidy and decorate it with flowers. She wanted to be able to spend time there.

But her dad had moved them here to Holly Hill. Her dad was giving money to a family friend who lived in their old village, so that *she* could buy the flowers and tend the grave instead.

Saf's dad had taken her away from the one place in the entire universe where she could still feel close to her mum.

'I'm sorry I shouted at you,' Saf said when they got back to the park.

'Don't worry about it,' Kevin replied. 'I'm sorry about your mum. Anyway, at least I know why you act so weird now.'

'Weirder than weird, that's me,' she smiled.

She was about to leave him and head home, when she stopped. Suddenly, she asked, 'Do you ever pray, Kevin?

Kevin was so startled by the question that for a moment he didn't know what to say. Then, 'Why?' he spluttered.

'Just thought you might, I suppose,' Saf shrugged. 'My mum asked me to pray for her,' she added quietly. 'Right before she died.'

'And did you?'

'I asked God to look after her. She was really ill so I suppose, in a way, He did.'

'That's all right, then,' said Kevin.
'Yeah,' nodded Saf.
And she got on her bike and cycled out of the park.

Five

Saf wasn't angry with God. She didn't blame Him for her mum getting ill. She didn't blame Him for the fact that her mum had died. It was just something that had happened. Something horrible and unfair. But it wasn't God's fault.

Just before that darkest day in Saf's whole life, she'd prayed on and off all night. Saf had never really talked to God before then. Not properly. Yes, when she was little in her Sunday School class, she'd said thank You for things like earthworms and flowers, and sunshine and people who love you. She'd joined in with the other small children, saying the Lord's Prayer and singing praise songs about butterflies' wings and fuzzy-wuzzy bears.

But in a way, it had all just been words; words she'd

spoken and sung because the others in the class were speaking and singing them, too. She'd never really taken it in that she was talking to a *real* God who was *really* listening. Of course, her mum had told her He was. But Saf never actually felt that *real*-ness for herself – until that last, long night.

'Pray for me,' Saf's mum had said. And that's what Saf did.

Can you hear me, God? Please hear me. It's very important, really important that You hear me, because my mum is ill and she's asked me to pray for her. So I need to be able to tell her that I have prayed and that You did hear me.

Thank You for giving me my mum and my dad and my little brother, Stevie. Thank You that we're a 'comfortably complete family of four'. Miss Mills at Sunday School used to say that when we talk to You, we should always begin by saying 'thank You' before we ask for anything. You've given us so much, she said, that it would be ungrateful to ask for more without thanking You for what we've got already. So I do thank You – I thank You so much for everything – but, please, I need to talk to You about my mum now.

My mum is wonderful. She really loves me. In fact, she says she loves the two of us (Stevie and me) so much that sometimes she thinks she'll burst. Stevie says he'll get a big shopping bag if that ever happens and then he'll be able to catch all the love as it whooshes out. Mum says a shopping bag wouldn't be big enough to hold it all. All that love. I think she's right.

Of course, Mum does get cross sometimes, too. She gets cross when Stevie and I argue about silly little things like what we watch on TV, or when we won't share stuff. She gets even crosser if we end up shouting or hitting each other. Stevie's bitten me before. Sometimes it's me who starts it. Sometimes it's Stevie. Mum says we have to say sorry to each other when we quarrel. 'Never let the sun go down on an argument,' she tells us.

'That's what it says in the Bible.' She means, don't go to bed at the end of the day still feeling cross with someone. But, of course, You'd know that, wouldn't You, being God.

One time I wouldn't say sorry to Stevie. I absolutely refused. Mum said it made her very sad. I didn't like upsetting her so in the end I said sorry to Stevie as soon as I could, which was a bit later that afternoon. I had to wait for him to come home from a birthday party.

One thing Mum's really good at is making cakes. I help her sometimes. I put the different things like the sugar and butter and flour into the mixing bowl. I cut out baking parchment and lay it in the bottom of the tins so that the cakes don't stick when it's time to get them out. I used to keep cutting the parchment the wrong size – too small so that it didn't fit the tins at all. Then Mum had this clever idea. She told me to stand the tin on the parchment and draw round it with a pencil. Now I could cut round the pencil line and the piece of parchment would fit the tin perfectly. I'd never have thought of that without Mum.

Mum says she can just about make a good cake, but is useless when it comes to jam. One year we picked blackberries. Loads of them. 'I'll make enough blackberry jam to last us till next year,' Mum said. But it went a bit wrong. It still looked all dark and purple and yummy, but it didn't go thick in the saucepan. So we ended up with a sort of blackberry dip instead of blackberry jam. 'Oh, never mind,' Mum said. 'We won't have it on toast. We'll pour it over ice cream. It'll be delicious.' So we did. And it was.

Mum thinks of the things no one else would think of, too. The kind things. On my first day at proper school, I was so scared. I told Mum I didn't want to go. I said couldn't I stay at home like usual and look at books and do jigsaws, and go for walks with her and find interesting things to bring home, like fallen leaves and empty snail shells and pretty feathers. Mum said it was time to do bigger things and I must be very brave. So I was brave and I went to school. And when I got home she gave me a cuddly toy rabbit. I called her Rachel. Rachel's my favourite toy. She always will be.

Mum never forgets things, either. Dad does. He never forgets important things like birthdays. But he does sometimes forget to take his library books back on the right date, and quite often he comes home with stuff missing from the shopping. 'Where are the potatoes?' Mum will ask. 'Oops,' Dad will answer. 'I knew there was something else.' Sometimes Mum gets a bit annoyed with him when that happens, but not for long. 'Oh, well,' she'll say. 'I suppose there are more important things to worry about than forgotten potatoes.' Dad says he's got a memory like a sieve. Mum agrees with him.

This prayer isn't about Dad, though. It's about Mum. You can see how special she is. Mum's the one who keeps our 'comfortably complete family of four' comfortable and complete. I love her so much, God, and it's all wrong that she's ill. Nothing's been the same since it started. Stevie and I have to be very quiet sometimes if she's in bed. And we have to try really hard not to argue – harder than usual, because Dad says

*the last thing Mum needs is to get upset because we're
squabbling. And Dad looks sad. Nearly all the time.*

*Sometimes when Mum's lying on the sofa, I sit there,
too, and read to her. I ask which story she'd like and she
chooses one. I hold the book so she can see the pictures.
But when I look round at her to see if she's enjoying the
story, she's fallen asleep. 'Hopeless, aren't I?' she always
says when she wakes up. 'You're not hopeless,' I say.
'You're just not feeling very well.' I always hope that the
next day she'll be feeling better. 'As a matter of fact, I
do feel a bit better this morning,' she might say when
I ask. But it doesn't change the fact that she's ill inside.
And the feeling better bit doesn't last.*

*So this is my prayer for my mum. I've never prayed a
prayer that's so long before. I've never prayed a prayer
that's so important before. This is the prayer Mum
asked for. This is the prayer I want You to hear, God,
more than any of the other words I've ever spoken.*

*When my granny died, (Mum's mum), I wasn't very old,
but I do remember Mum being really sad. 'I shouldn't be
sad,' she said. 'Granny loved God, and now she's gone to
be with Him. She was ill, and now she's not ill any more.'*

*That's what I want for my mum. That's what I'm asking
You for, God. When Mum's with You, I'm asking for her
not to be ill any more either. She doesn't deserve to be ill.
Please look after her. Please never stop looking after her.*

The night of Saf's prayer, she'd talked and talked to
God. Her mum had told her He was always there; always

listening; always ready to help when anyone asked Him for help. 'Whenever you've got something to say to God,' her mum had said, 'just say it.'

So Saf had sat there in the dark and said everything. And for the first time, she really had known God was there, listening to every word. Not that she'd heard Him breathing, or fidgeting, or going, 'Mmm,' when she said something He especially agreed with. He was just there.

A hand holding hers in the darkness.

Keeping her company.

Saf treasured that time. A time for just her and God. Why was it, then, she often wondered in the months after her mum had died, that she hadn't spoken to God since?

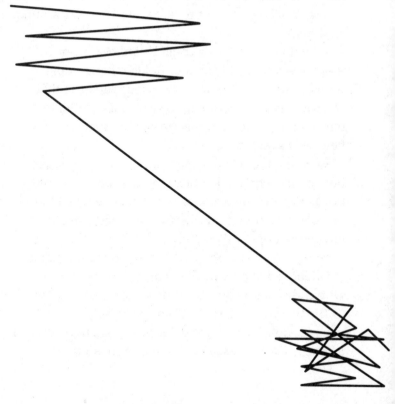

Six

'Hi, Saf!'

Saf whirled around, startled. She was standing in the queue for the checkout in the corner shop. Her dad had asked her to go and buy some milk.

'Blue top, please, Saf,' he grinned. 'Can't have coffee without my full fat blue top.'

Stevie wanted to go, too, but Pete wasn't happy to let Saf be in charge of him on her own in the town. Not quite yet anyway.

'When we've been here a little bit longer, eh?' he said. 'The roads are so much busier than where we used to live, Stevie. I just want to let Saf find her way around a bit first.'

Saf didn't mind. Stevie could be annoying when they were out; difficult about holding hands; doing silly walking; running off in the supermarket so that you spent more time trying to keep track of him than getting the shopping done. He would usually listen to Pete. He never listened to Saf.

Saf stood there in the checkout queue, one finger hooked through the handle of a blue-topped, plastic bottle of milk. She was lost in thought. So when the boy behind her said his cheerful, 'Hi, Saf!', she almost jumped out of her skin.

'Sorry,' he mumbled, 'didn't mean to scare you.'

Saf looked at him. He was a bit taller than she was, with curly, blond hair almost down to his shoulders.

The boy went on, slightly uncomfortably, 'Actually, you probably haven't got a clue who I am, have you? I'm a Topz ... That is to say, I'm John and I'm a Topz. In the

Topz Gang. With Sarah. I'm her brother ... We met at – '

'Sunday Club, I know,' Saf interrupted. 'I remember.'

'Right ... Anyway, I just wanted to say hello.'

John paused awkwardly. This wasn't strictly true. He hadn't really wanted to speak to Saf at all. He'd spotted her a short way in front of him as he'd walked to the shop with Gruff. His mum had asked him to pop out for milk, too. He could have caught her up, but he hung back. He wasn't sure what to say; what they could talk about if they walked the rest of the way together. After all, Saf had been very quiet at Sunday Club. She didn't seem to want to be there. It was bound to end up feeling difficult for both of them. He'd leave it for another time, he thought. She wasn't likely to notice him anyway.

Only then, of course, Saf had gone into the shop ahead of him. It wouldn't be so easy to avoid her in there. Anyway, John couldn't help thinking about the prayer they'd all been praying – *God, please help us know how to talk to Saf. Please give us just the right words at the right time.*

That's when he knew he shouldn't try and avoid her, however uncomfortable it felt. How could he even have a go at saying the right words if he didn't have a conversation with her in the first place?

The checkout queue was shifting. It was almost Saf's turn to pay.

'I wish we were allowed blue top milk,' John said quickly, glancing at the bottle still dangling from her finger. 'We have to have semi-skimmed. Sometimes even totally skimmed depending on how excited Mum is about her keeping fit thing. I mean, have you ever had totally skimmed milk? Honestly, you may as well just put water on your cornflakes.'

John stopped suddenly. What was he babbling on about? Skimmed milk? Surely God couldn't want him to be talking to Saf about skimmed milk! But at the same time, just for a moment, he was sure he saw her try and hide a smile.

As Saf finished paying and he stepped forward with his semi-skimmed bottle, John thought, it's now or never.

'If you're going home, I'll walk back with you,' he offered, fishing in his pocket for some money.

It was Saf's turn to feel awkward. She felt as if there were people looking at her. She didn't know how to get out of it.

'OK,' she nodded.

Outside the shop, a small, greyish-brown dog was sitting patiently on the pavement. He jumped up the moment he saw John in the shop doorway.

'This is Gruff,' John said, unlooping the dog's lead from the newspaper stand where he'd tied him up. 'You're all right with dogs, are you?' he added, in case Saf might be nervous of them.

'I love dogs,' she smiled. She crouched down to Gruff,

whose stubby little tail was wagging backwards and forwards so fast it was making a draft. He put his front feet up on Saf's knees so that the two of them were almost nose to nose. It made Saf laugh.

'He's gorgeous,' she giggled.

'Yeah, he's OK most of the time,' nodded John. 'I mean, he's scruffy, noisy, makes a *real* mess and hardly ever stops eating, but … come to think of it, that's just like me! We've got a cat, too. Well, Sarah's got a cat. She's called Saucy.'

'You're so lucky,' Saf replied, scratching Gruff's ears while he panted excitedly. His tongue kept flopping out of his mouth. 'I always wanted a pet. I was going to get a rabbit only … well, then we sort of had to move here so it didn't happen.'

'That's a shame,' said John. 'You could still get one, though. Paul's dad – Paul's in Topz, too – is totally brilliant at DIY. He can build anything. I bet he could make you a hutch.'

'Thanks, but I don't know if Dad wants any animals now.'

'Well, you can always come with me when I take Gruff for a walk,' John went on. He was feeling more relaxed now they had something to talk about. 'And you should come round to our house and meet Saucy. Sarah won't mind. She'll love it.' He hesitated, but only for a second. 'You can come round now if you want. We could ask your dad if it's all right on the way there. My house isn't far from yours.'

For the second time that morning, Saf wasn't sure how to answer. But before she had time to say anything, a pair of trainer-clad feet stopped on the pavement beside her.

John instantly took a step backwards.

'I've been looking for you, Saf.' It was Kevin. 'Never thought I'd find you chatting to a Topz.'

Saf straightened up, carefully placing Gruff's paws back on the pavement.

'It's not up to you who I talk to, is it, Kevin?' she retorted. 'Anyway I was just going home. I only stopped to say hello to the dog.'

'You talk to dogs?' Kevin smirked.

'Of course I do,' Saf replied. 'Why wouldn't I?'

John stood there silently. He seemed tense now. Nervous, almost. Not at all like the boy who'd just been making her laugh.

'Got to go, John, sorry,' Saf said.

'It's fine,' John murmured.

'Thanks for letting me say hello to Gruff.'

'It's fine,' he said again. 'I'm sure we'll … see you around.'

He watched Saf as she started to walk back up the street, with Kevin trailing just slightly behind. How had they got to know each other? Couldn't Saf see Dixons were the wrong gang to be hanging around with? Didn't she know how dangerous they were?

John knew. He knew because he'd got himself into trouble with them not long before. You kept away from Dixons if you knew what was good for you. He wanted to shout after Saf, 'You don't have to do anything you don't want to do, you know!'

But he didn't. He watched them disappear round the corner, then he and Gruff made their own way home.

'I'll meet you at the park later,' Kevin had said when they got to the end of Saf's road. 'I've got something to show you.'

Saf couldn't imagine what Kevin wanted her to see. Unless it was something to do with his dad's grave. Maybe he'd tidied it up at long last.

'I'll be at the park, or somewhere round there,' she told her dad as she went to get her bike after lunch. 'And, yes, I promise I won't start riding until I get there.'

But this time, Pete picked her up on something else. 'What do you mean "somewhere round there"? Where else might you go?'

'Nowhere,' Saf answered, irritated. 'I'll be around the park.'

'Well, please make sure you're back by half past four,' Pete insisted. 'We're going round to Auntie Becky's, remember.'

When Saf got to the park, Kevin was waiting for her. She found him sitting on the roundabout, pushing himself slowly around with the toe of one trainer. He scrambled off when he saw her but he didn't smile.

'Thought you were never going to get here,' he grumbled.

'Are you still cross because I talked to that Topz boy?' Saf frowned.

'I told you, Topz and Dixons don't mix.'

'And I told you,' Saf answered back, 'I don't want to be friends with Topz, but I think they're OK. If I want to talk to them, I'll talk to them.'

Kevin scowled and started kicking moodily at the roundabout.

'You'll ruin your trainers doing that,' Saf remarked.

He looked at her in disbelief. 'You sound just like my mum.'

Saf couldn't help smiling at that. It broke the mood and Kevin grinned, too.

'So,' Saf said, 'what did you want to show me?'

'Well, it's not here, is it? Let's go.'

'Go where? I can't go far, I told Dad I'd be around the park.'

Kevin was already walking towards the main gates. 'It *is* around the park, sort of,' he grunted over his shoulder.

'Around the park where?' Saf wanted to know, starting to push her bike after him. He always walked so quickly.

'Follow me and you'll find out!'

Where Kevin led Saf was actually nowhere near the park at all. It must have been about as far away as the cemetery.

Kevin took her to the Dixons Estate.

Seven

'Why have we stopped here?'

Saf stood uncertainly in front of a building site at the end of Rock Road. It was fenced off with high, metal mesh panels.

Behind the fencing stood a large, square, ugly, four-storey building. At least, Saf thought it was ugly. It was meant to have been a new block of flats for the Dixons Estate. The plan was to have gardens surrounding it. Nothing too fancy, just stretches of grass divided into rectangles with paving slab paths, and a few bushes and willow trees. The greenness would help soften the look of the new flats once they were completed.

But in the end, they'd never been finished. Something went wrong and the builder's money ran out. Work had stopped weeks ago, just after the roof went on. The building was still little more than a shell. Walls gaped with empty windows and doorways. It was damp inside, too, where the rain blew in. Just miserable, Saf thought, scanning the DANGER – KEEP OUT signs that had been put up in several obvious places.

She was puzzled. 'Why have you brought me to this dump?'

'It's not a dump. Anyway, I told you,' Kevin replied bluntly, 'I've got something to show you.' He shot a glance over his shoulder. There was no one around. But then there hardly ever was at this end of Rock Road. 'Come on.'

He led Saf down the side of the unfinished flats, following the line of the fence. The ground underfoot was very uneven, heaped with rubbish from all the building work. Saf struggled with her bike, stumbling on the loose stones and piles of earth tufted with grass. Kevin didn't offer to help. He didn't even seem to notice she was having trouble.

As soon as they were out of sight of Rock Road, Kevin said, 'You can leave your bike here.'

Saf shook her head. 'I don't want to leave it here. I'll take it with me.'

'You can't.'

'Why not?'

'Because we're climbing over the fence.'

Saf blinked at him. 'We're doing what?'

'You heard,' Kevin grunted. He saw the doubt flicker across her face. 'What's the problem? It's not as if anyone lives here.'

Saf nodded towards one of the signs just above their heads. 'It says "KEEP OUT".'

'So?'

'Well, we're not supposed to go in there, are we?'

'Yeah and ...?' Kevin shrugged. '*I* do,' he said.
'All the time.'

'But ... what if someone sees?'

'They won't. I told you, no one lives here, no one comes here. Besides,' he added, turning and planting one foot on the fence, 'if it belongs to anyone, it belongs to Dixons now. This is our den.'

With that, he swung his other foot forward. Then he pushed himself upwards and clawed his way up the metal mesh of the fence with his fingers. In no time he was over the top and standing on the other side. Saf could hardly believe her eyes.

'So,' he said, hands on hips, 'are you coming, or what?'

'How do you expect me to do that?' she gasped. 'That fence is massive.'

Kevin's shoulders hunched up in another shrug. 'If you don't do it, you won't get in.'

Saf stared at him. Then, looking round to make completely sure there was no one watching, she lowered her bike to the ground and put one foot on the fence.

'Now you just climb,' Kevin said.

It wasn't as easy as he had made it look. Saf was smaller than he was; much lighter, too. But her arms weren't very strong and hauling herself up was a huge effort. At the top she wavered. The fence was tall but from up here, the ground seemed further away than she was expecting.

'This is so high!' she squealed.

'You've just got to jump, Saf,' Kevin told her impatiently.

'I can't!'

'Just jump!'

It was partly a jump; partly a twist; partly a tumble. But somehow or other Saf ended up on the other side of the fence, the right way up and even on her feet.

'Told you,' Kevin grinned. 'You've just got to jump.'

Saf's heart was thudding, but Kevin didn't give her a moment to catch her breath. He'd already turned away and was walking towards the corner of the building. She ran after him.

Round the back was a double door opening. If the flats were ever finished, this would be a fire escape. Two doors would be fixed in here, with glass in the top half of each, and push-down bars across the middle to open them. But for the moment, of course, there was nothing.

Kevin stepped through the opening and into the building. Then he turned to face Saf, a smug smile creeping across his face.

'Well, this is it,' he announced, spreading his arms. 'Dixons' Den.'

Saf peered in through the doorway. There was another door opening to her left, with a corridor leading away from it. Other than that, the space where Kevin stood was just an empty square surrounded by four blank walls. Empty, that is, apart from the staircase right in front of them. It was grey and cold-looking. Like the one in the multi-storey car park at the shopping centre.

'Is this … what you wanted to show me?' Saf asked slowly.

'Yup,' Kevin answered. 'What do you think?'

Saf wasn't sure what to say. 'Why do you come here?' she mumbled finally. 'I mean … what do you do?'

'We just hang about. What else do you do in a den?'

Suddenly he was on the move again. He leapt up the stairs two at a time, turning at the top of the first flight to call, 'Well, come on, then.'

Saf was feeling even more nervous now. She shook her head. 'I'm not sure. How do you know it's safe?'

'Of course it's safe,' Kevin snapped, a little disappointed that Saf didn't seem more impressed with Dixons' Den. 'It's concrete.'

And he was gone. Saf could hear his trainers slapping on the hard surface of each step as he climbed higher and higher above her. She didn't want to follow him up. But she didn't want to be left on her own standing in the doorway of an empty building either. Taking two stairs at a time just as he had, she raced up behind him.

There were eight flights of steps altogether, each one separated by a small landing. They led all the way up to the fourth floor at the top of the building. Each floor had a doorway from the staircase opening onto a corridor, the same as where they'd come in from outside.

Saf was out of breath when she reached the top. 'Do you ever go in there?' she puffed, nodding at the door opening.

'Yup, sometimes,' Kevin nodded. 'It's just rooms, but there's nowhere to sit. The stairs are better.'

As if to prove it, he slumped down on the top step, pulling her down beside him. 'See? Comfy as anything.'

Saf made a face. 'Like you said, Kevin, it's concrete. There's nothing comfy about concrete. It's all dirty for a start, and it's *dead* cold!'

She got back onto her feet and started brushing a chalky-looking dust from the back of her jeans.

That's when she heard it.

A noise from downstairs.

Saf froze, listening.

'What?' asked Kevin.

'Sssh!'

$Sssh!$

There it was again! This time they both heard it.

There was someone else in the building.

Saf caught her breath and twisted her head towards Kevin. 'Did you hear that?' she hissed. 'That was footsteps. You said no one ever comes here!'

'They don't.'

'Well, clearly someone has, I can hear them!'

'I told you,' Kevin answered, not seeming worried in the slightest. 'This is Dixons' Den. The only people who come here are Dixons.'

'That's right,' said a voice. It wasn't friendly.

Saf whirled around. Two boys were standing at the foot of the flight of stairs in front of her.

'And if the only people who come here are Dixons,' the boy who'd spoken went on, 'then what I want to know is – what do you think *you're* doing here?'

Saf felt a prickle of fear creeping up her spine. This was different from the last time she'd seen Dixons. Then, they'd been in the park. It was wide open there with other people milling about. She hadn't been scared of them then, not really. Why should she be?

But this wasn't the same at all. This time it was just Saf and Dixons.

This time she was on their territory.

Saf swallowed hard. 'I – ' she began, but behind her, Kevin had already jumped to his feet.

'*I* brought her, Clyde,' he said cheerfully.

'I knew it!' scowled Rick. 'When we saw her bike down there, didn't I say I bet she came here with Kevin!'

'What's going on, Kev?' Clyde demanded as he strode up the last few stairs. 'This is our place. Dixons'. You've got no business bringing someone else here. We agreed, remember?'

Kevin looked annoyed. 'We agreed not to tell anyone we come here,' he retorted. 'That's different. Anyway, Saf's OK. She won't tell anyone, will you?'

Saf didn't get the chance to answer. Rick was suddenly standing right in front of her. He stared down his nose nastily, dark eyes peering out from under his scruffy fringe.

'She'd better not, that's all,' he snarled.

He was too close to her, Saf thought. Much too close. She wanted to step away from him ... but no. That's what he was waiting for, wasn't it? For her to back off; run away. These Dixons wanted to feel as if they were in complete control.

Well, Saf wanted some control, too. She was sick of being pushed around. She felt she'd had more than enough of that in the last few months. And it wasn't as if these other two boys would hurt her, would they, with Kevin there? No. Just because they were bullies, that didn't mean she had to let them bully *her*. So she stood her ground.

Almost immediately, Kevin barged his way between the two of them.

'Look, Rick,' he grunted, 'I told you she won't say anything, and she *won't say anything*!'

Rick was the one who backed off.

'What's wrong with you, Kev?' muttered Clyde. 'You're acting really weird now you've got yourself a girlfriend.'

Girlfriend? Saf wasn't impressed. 'I'm not his girlfriend!'

she snapped. 'I'm not anyone's girlfriend!'

The three Dixons boys stared at her. They weren't used to anyone standing up to them. This girl might be small but, as Kevin had already discovered, she wasn't afraid to speak her mind.

'What is it you want, Kevin?' Clyde demanded. 'She's not joining Dixons, if that's what you're after.'

'I wouldn't join Dixons if you *begged* me to,' Saf retorted.

'Well, we're *not* begging you to, are we?' Kevin replied abruptly. He glanced from Rick to Clyde. 'I just thought she could come here sometimes, that's all. It's boring going to the park all the time. I thought Saf could share our den.'

'Why?' asked Rick.

'Because I want her to!'

There was a pause. Dixons eyed each other. Then a smirk slowly twisted the corners of Clyde's mouth.

'OK,' he nodded. 'She can share our den. On one condition.'

'What condition?' frowned Kevin.

Yes, what condition? wondered Saf. No one had even asked her if she *wanted* to share the den. And she wished they wouldn't keep talking about her as if she wasn't there.

Clyde's eyes flicked meaningfully towards Rick. 'She'll have to pass the test, won't she, Rick?'

For a moment, Rick looked blank. Then he realised what Clyde meant and he started to grin, too.

'What are you on about?' Kevin wanted to know. 'What test?'

'The test,' Clyde repeated, this time staring straight at Saf. 'Let's see how fast she can run.'

Eight

A mobile rang. It made Saf jump.

Awkwardly, she reached into the pocket of her jeans and pulled it out.

'Hello?'

'Hi, Saf,' said her dad, 'just checking you haven't forgotten the time. You will be back by half past four, won't you?'

Saf glanced at the clock on her phone. It was nearly quarter to four already.

'Of course I will,' she mumbled.

'Only Uncle Nick's doing a barbecue and we mustn't be late.'

'OK,' she replied. 'I'll be back.'

Glancing up, she found all three pairs of Dixons' eyes fixed on her. 'I've got to go in a minute,' she muttered quietly.

'Oh, dear,' said Rick sarcastically. 'What a shame.'

Clyde folded his arms. 'No, hang on. Don't you even want to know what the test is?'

'It's easy, Saf,' said Kevin, who'd worked out what Clyde was getting at. 'It's just a bit of a laugh, that's all.'

'All right, then, what is it?' Saf asked, not really sure if she wanted to know or not.

'It's a time trial,' Clyde explained. 'We do lots of them. We run up and down all these stairs, one of us at a time, top to the bottom and back again. Fastest one wins.'

Saf glanced at the staircase behind Clyde. '*All* these stairs? Right down to the ground floor?'

'Yup.'

'But there's loads of them.'

'Exactly,' nodded Kevin. 'That's why it makes a good time trial.'

Tearing up and down your own stairs at home as fast as you could had to be a little bit dangerous, Saf thought. Tearing up and down *these* stairs was just stupid. They were concrete! It couldn't really be a good idea, could it?

Still, she wasn't going to say that to Dixons.

'So,' challenged Clyde, his arms still folded across his chest, 'you up for it? Because, if you're faster than all of us, then you can come and use the den. But if you're not, well … you'll have to make your own den somewhere else.'

'That's not fair,' grumbled Kevin.

'No?' answered Clyde. 'Well, that's the way it is, Kev. And you know you shouldn't have brought her here in the first place.'

'I'm not sure,' Saf said quietly. 'That was my dad on the phone. I've got to go in a minute, I can't be late.'

'Well, if you run *really* fast, you won't have to be late, will you?' Rick sneered. 'Or is running up and down all these stairs too much for a little girl like you?'

That was all it took to make up Saf's mind.

'I can do anything you can do,' she snapped. '*And* my hair will never look as bad as yours!'

Rick was about to answer back, but the other two boys burst out laughing, so he thought better of it. 'OK,' he muttered instead. 'Game on.
Who's going first?'

Once again, all eyes were on Saf. She shook her head. 'No. I want to see one of you do it before I go.'

'Me, then,' Rick said, undoing his watch and handing

it to Kevin. It had a timer on it. 'Can't wait to beat you, little girl.'

He pushed through the others and stood at the top of the staircase.

'You ready?' asked Kevin.

'Yup.' Rick tossed his head to shake his fringe out of his eyes, clenching and unclenching his fists. Then he tensed, ready to run.

'Go!' Kevin shouted. At the same time, he jabbed his thumb into the timer button on the watch. The seconds started to count down.

Saf watched, amazed, as Rick hurled himself downwards. He didn't hold the banister. Keeping close to the wall all the way down, he used his left hand against the rough, grey blocks to steady himself. And he was fast. *Really* fast. He'd hardly reached the bottom before he was tearing back up again – two steps at a time – landing back on the top floor with a triumphant spring. He punched the air as he gasped for breath.

'Fast enough for you, little girl?' he panted, grinning all over his face.

Saf just looked at him. She was even more worried now, although she'd never let him see. How could she do what he'd just done? Surely she'd fall on the first flight.

'Not bad,' nodded Kevin. 'Thirty-eight seconds. Think you were faster last time, though, weren't you?'

'Who cares? As long as I'm faster than her.' Rick jerked his head in Saf's direction.

'Me next,' said Clyde.

He got himself into position and, 'Go!' shouted Kevin again.

Clyde shot off. Just like Rick, he kept close to the wall

as he tore up and down. And just like Rick, he was very, very fast.

'Thirty-nine,' announced Kevin.

'Let me see that,' puffed Clyde, not at all happy it had taken him longer than Rick. He reached out and grabbed the watch, peering at the figures on the dial. 'You sure you didn't press the button early?'

'Of course I didn't press the button early,' retorted Kevin. 'I'm not stupid.'

Then he looked at Saf. 'You next or me?' he asked.

'Don't care,' Saf answered sharply.

She did care, though. She cared that she'd let herself in for this at all. What was she thinking? She'd never beat the boys in a million years. After all, if they did this all the time, they were bound to be faster than she was.

Then there was that other thing. The voice inside her convincing her she'd fall and break her neck. It wasn't as if she even wanted to be able to use the den. She just didn't want Rick to win; didn't want Rick or any of them thinking they were better than she was.

Rick snatched his watch back and Kevin went next. He was quick, too. Quick enough to put him in the lead. Thirty-six seconds it took him and he looked really smug. Saf couldn't work out why. He wanted her to be able to use the den, but now he'd made it even more unlikely that she'd be able to beat the Dixons' fastest time. How could she possibly run up and down that staircase in under thirty-six seconds?

Saf's mum used to say, 'When you're faced with something you don't want to do, the best thing is not to think about it too much. Just put your head down and get on with it.'

She wouldn't have said that about this, of course. Saf's mum would have been horrified. Horrified that her darling girl was even thinking about charging headlong up and down a concrete staircase. Horrified that Saf was on the wrong side of a **'DANGER – KEEP OUT'** sign. Horrified that she'd got herself mixed up with boys like Dixons. Not that she wouldn't have cared about them, or been kind to them, or tried to like them. Saf's mum would have done all those things. But what she wouldn't have wanted, with every last breath in her body, was for Saf to get hurt trying to prove herself.

As Saf stood on the top step, she could feel Rick's eyes burning into her. His thumb hovered eagerly over the timer button on his watch. He couldn't wait for her to go; couldn't wait for her to fail; couldn't wait for her to fall, probably.

Kevin and Clyde were waiting, too. Just behind her.

Then there was her dad waiting for her at home. He thought she was at the park. If someone told him where she was right now, he'd never believe it. Whatever was the time now? At any moment, her phone could ring again, with Pete grumbling crossly, 'Saf, what are you playing at? I told you to be home by half past four!'

She *wanted* to be at home. She wanted to feel safe.

But she had to run. Dixons couldn't win. They'd be bound to have beaten her time already, that was obvious. She could never be as fast as they were, not first time round. But they couldn't beat her into backing out of a challenge. She just had to –

'GO!' yelled Rick.

And Saf ran.

Her feet began to pound on the stairs. Her left hand grazed the grey wall as she tore her way down, following the line the boys had taken. She wasn't really aware of her legs. She couldn't think about what they were doing; couldn't make them try and go faster. She just had to let them run and run. Down and down.

Were Dixons still watching her from the top?

Could they still see her?

Saf hadn't a clue which floor she was on until suddenly she saw the door to outside. A waft of fresh air blew in as she jumped the last few steps. But she landed awkwardly, falling over slightly on her ankle, although if it hurt she didn't feel it. She didn't have time to feel it.

As she whirled round to start the climb back up again, she stumbled, losing her balance slightly. In an instant, she recovered herself and sprang onto the stairs. Up and up. Her mouth was so dry she couldn't swallow. She couldn't catch her breath! Her lungs felt as if they were trying to burst out of her chest.

And at last, there they were. The three Dixons boys all standing in a line at the very top.

'Come on, Saf!' Kevin shouted.

Almost on the last stair, Saf's legs gave up on her. She tripped and plunged forward. Hurtling into Clyde, she knocked him backwards with the pair of them ending up in a heap against the wall.

Clyde shoved her away. 'Get off me!'

Saf was left on her hands and knees. She gasped for breath. It felt as if there'd never be enough air in the whole world to give her lungs what they were screaming for. It wasn't just the effort of running. Saf was fit. Fitter than Dixons, probably.

It was the fear.

The fear of falling.

The fear of ending up all broken at the bottom of the concrete stairs.

The fear of doing something she shouldn't be doing, somewhere she had no business being.

Fear had completely taken her **breath away.**

Nine

Saf's dad had told her to be home on time because Uncle Nick and Auntie Becky were doing a barbecue. What he hadn't said was that Rhianna had invited the whole of the Topz Gang.

It was three minutes after half past four when Saf shot in through the back door.

'Sorry, sorry!' she mumbled.

She didn't wait for Pete to tell her she was late or ask why she looked in such a state. She rushed straight upstairs calling, 'I'll be ready in a minute. I'll just have a wash.'

Saf felt boiling hot. In the bathroom, she stood by the basin and turned on the cold tap. She pushed back her fringe and let the water run across her palms. Then she leaned forward and splashed handfuls over her face. It was cool and made her skin tingle; washing away the dust from the building site; the sweat from the time trial.

Saf hoped it would wash away the fear, too.

It didn't.

As she reached for her towel and raised her head, she caught sight of her face in the mirror. Her blue-grey eyes gazed back at her. They were like her mum's eyes, everyone said, but perhaps slightly more blue.

Right now there was a question in them: *what do you think you're doing, playing dangerous games with dangerous boys?*

Going to the building site wasn't the only wrong thing Saf had done that afternoon. There was something else. Something her dad always told her not to do whenever she went out on her bike. Saf was so afraid she'd be late home that she'd ridden it along the busy streets, all the way from the Dixons Estate to the end of their road in Holly Hill.

But riding her bike outside the park wasn't just about being late. In the end, Saf couldn't get away from Dixons' Den quick enough.

Dixons had laughed at her after her time trial.

'Forty-two seconds!' Rick yelled delightedly, almost crushing the timer button on his watch as he stopped the count. 'Slow or what!'

Even Kevin had sniggered. He was so proud of his own thirty-six-second run.

'And today's winner is ... KEVIN!' he crowed, doing a stupid little victory dance on the top landing.

'Which means, of course,' declared Clyde, a harsh glint in his eyes, 'that your girlfriend needs to get out of Dixons' Den. Now.'

Saf had managed to scramble shakily to her feet after stumbling over at the top of the staircase. But she still had to steady herself against the wall. Her legs were trembling so much, she felt they might give way at any moment.

'Oh, come on, Clyde,' she heard Kevin say. 'Who cares if she wasn't the fastest? Why can't we just let her come here if she wants?'

'Because rules are rules, Kev,' Rick butted in. 'Fastest time or nothing.' He turned and glared at Saf spitefully. 'Sorry, little girl. But this is a "Dixons only" den. And it always will be.'

There was silence. Just for a moment, no one said a word. Not even Kevin.

Then Saf was running again. Down and down the stairs.

Right down to the ground floor and outside. Her legs were still shaking. Her whole body shook. But she had to get out and away.

Climbing back over the fence seemed easier this time, in spite of her shakiness. The urge to escape from Dixons kept pushing her up and on.

There was her bike on the other side. Once back on Rock Road, she had never pedalled so fast in all her life …

'Saf, please hurry up! We're going to be late!' Pete's voice calling up the stairs to the bathroom was far from happy.

'Coming,' Saf replied.

She looked at herself in the mirror once more. It had been a horrible afternoon. The worst since they'd arrived in Holly Hill. But weirdly, there was something – some strange sensation – deep in the pit of her stomach that was almost making her feel better. Just a tiny bit.

Ever since her mum had died, Saf had felt helpless. Everything was decided for her. All the time. What she wanted didn't seem important at all. Not to anyone. Least of all to her dad.

But this afternoon, she'd been somewhere and done something her dad knew nothing about. It was *her* decision to go with Kevin – certainly the worst decision ever and it had scared her to death – but it was a decision *she'd* made. All on her own.

In a very odd way, it gave her a feeling of freedom.

That's why she kept looking in the mirror. Saf could see something that looked like freedom in her face.

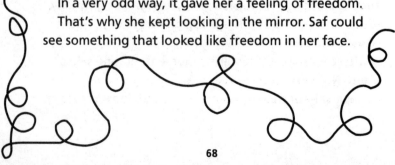

When Pete, Saf and Stevie arrived for Uncle Nick's barbecue, Saf's heart sank like a stone in a pond.

'Hi, Saf,' chirped Rhianna, far too cheerfully Saf thought. 'I've got a surprise for you. Remember Topz?'

And there they all were; the whole Topz Gang, running up to say hello.

Pete spotted Saf's dismayed expression, but all he said was, 'Thought it might be nice for you to spend some time with your friends.'

'Yeah!' squealed Stevie. 'Paul's got a go-cart! He told me.'

'They're *not* my friends,' Saf wanted to retort. But she didn't. She didn't say a word.

'Are you settling in a bit better now, Saf?' Josie asked.

'I'm fine,' she answered.

'Goes out on her bike loads, don't you?' said Rhianna. 'You must be so fit!'

'I like cycling.'

'If you ever want to go ice skating, we sometimes go,' invited Benny. 'You have to not mind falling over, though. I fall over lots, and I don't mind one bit!'

Saf shook her head. 'I don't really like falling over,' she muttered. 'I told you, I like cycling.'

'Oh, we have cycling trips, too,' Benny went on, eagerly. 'Sometimes we go with Sunday Club. Sometimes it's just Topz.'

'And if you ever want a ride on a go-kart,' added Paul, 'I've got one.'

'I know,' Saf replied flatly. 'I heard Stevie say.'

It was obvious that Saf didn't want to chat. If this was some cunning plan of her dad's to get her 'into' Topz, it was never going to work.

Later, when everyone was in the back garden, clustered around the barbecue, Saf wandered round to the front of the house. She sat on the wall by the road and kicked her heels against the brickwork. That's where John found her.

'You didn't know Topz were all going to be here, did you?' he smiled sympathetically.

'Not really,' Saf answered.

'I guess we can be a bit much all in one go. Anyway … I thought you might like a burger.' John held out a plate that was mostly hidden by the enormous, puffy bun sandwich sitting on it. Tomato sauce oozed from the sides. 'I asked for fried onions on it. Don't know whether you like onions, though. And there's probably far too much ketchup. Sarah always moans at me because I put so much on. "Why do you always have to drown a perfectly good burger in too much tomato sauce?" she says.' He paused awkwardly. 'You don't have to eat it if you don't want to.'

'No,' Saf said. 'It looks nice. Thanks,' and she took the plate.

Saf didn't really know why, but she quite liked John. Perhaps it was because he had a dog.

'How's Gruff?' she asked.

'He's fine. Well, bananas as usual, but fine.'

'Good. And … what's your cat called?'

'Saucy,' John reminded her. 'She's not mine, she's Sarah's. She's fine, too. Saucy, that is, not Sarah. I mean, Sarah is fine, obviously … because she's here … at the barbecue. But, I was talking about Saucy being fine when I said, "She's fine" …' John trailed off.

That's when he realised Saf was smiling at him.

'Sorry,' he muttered. 'I'm rambling, aren't I? That's another thing Sarah moans at me for.'

'I don't mind,' grinned Saf. 'I've been known to ramble myself.'

By the time she'd munched her way through her enormous burger, the two of them were chatting quite easily. There was something kind about John. So open, too. If she asked him, Saf had the feeling he'd tell her everything there was to know about himself.

'Do you ever feel free, John?' Saf asked suddenly.

'What?' They'd been laughing and joking. John wasn't expecting Saf to ask something so serious.

'You know, do you ever feel free to do just what you want to? To be exactly who you want to be?'

John thought for a moment. 'I can't do *exactly* what I want,' he said slowly. 'I mean, there are days when I'd like to turn Sarah into a lizard, but that's never going to happen. Or I'd like my bedroom to have a purple ceiling, but I just know Mum would never go for it. And most of the time I'd rather do *anything* instead of my homework, but I suppose homework's got to be done. So, no, I can't do just what I want. Who can? But … I think I'm *being* who I want to be. Why? Aren't you?'

Saf wasn't smiling any more, John noticed.

'I don't know,' she replied quietly. 'I'm not really sure who I am. I didn't want to move here, but I had to anyway. And now we're here, it feels as if Dad's just expecting me to fit in with everything *he* wants for me – rather than anything being what *I* want.'

Saf paused. Her visit to Dixons' Den was still fresh in her mind. Still horrible, but at the same time, still giving her that tiny sense of freedom. If she could tell anyone about it, she could tell John. But then again, if she talked about it – if it didn't stay her secret – the feeling of freedom might go away. As sure as anything, John would tell her never to go there again.

John was watching her, waiting for her to carry on talking. She didn't. And inside John's head, the words of Topz' prayer kept running round and round; the prayer they'd all agreed to pray for Saf: *God, please help us to say the right words to Saf at just the right time so we can help her.*

But what was the right thing to say? Right there, right now?

'I need you to help me, God.' John murmured it under his breath. Too quietly for Saf to hear, but John knew that God would. God heard everything. The tiniest thought.

'The thing is ...' he began, 'it's really awful what's happened to you, Saf. I'm so sorry about your mum. All of Topz are. I know we're a bit loud and stupid sometimes, but ... Anyway, the thing about being free to be myself is that, I suppose I want to be what God wants me to be. The Bible says He knows me inside out. He knows what I'm good at and what I'm rubbish at. So, I guess, because He knows me so well, He knows the best way for me to be happy. That's what makes me feel completely free – because I know that He loves me and made me the way I am.'

Saf was gazing out towards the road. Had she even listened to him? John couldn't be sure.

'Saf,' he went on suddenly. He had to say something, and this might be his only chance. 'Saf, I know you see Kevin sometimes. I don't know about the other Dixons, but I know you see Kevin. It's none of my business, really, only … be careful. I know what Dixons are like. Talk to *me* if you need a friend. Talk to Rhianna, or any of Topz. Best of all, talk to God. God wants what's best for you. The very best. **Dixons don't.'**

Saf knew John was right. Her mum had told her to talk to God. And when she got around to talking to Him again, Saf knew He'd hear her. He'd heard her those few months ago, just before her mum had died. He'd hear her again, she was sure of it.

'I know what Dixons are like,' John had warned.

But Saf thought she knew what they were like, too. And she didn't want to be friends with them. Not even Kevin, really, not after this afternoon.

What Saf wanted was to beat them. She wanted to beat them in a time trial on the concrete stairs at the building site. She wanted to run up and down those steps so fast that the smug grins on their sneering faces would drop right off onto the concrete floor!

She'd do it, too. She'd make absolutely sure of it.

No one would know – not her dad, not Dixons, and definitely not John. But Saf would sneak back to the unfinished flats at the end of Rock Road as often as she could when she was sure Dixons weren't there. She'd tear up and down the stairs all on her own, over and over again. She'd pace herself, time herself and get a proper rhythm going with her feet.

And when she was fast enough, she'd challenge Dixons to another time trial.

They'd never look down their noses at her and call her 'little girl' ever again. She'd free herself from them

by being better than they were.
Then Saf would be the winner.
Or so she thought.

Ten

'I'm going for a walk, Dad,' Saf called, slipping into her trainers by the back door.

'Can I come, too?' piped Stevie, running into the kitchen after her.

Pete appeared in the doorway. 'Have you given up cycling?' he asked. 'You never take your bike any more.'

'I just feel like walking. What's wrong with that?'

'Nothing,' Pete shrugged. 'I'm only saying, that's all.'

Stevie was jumping up and down. 'Can I go, Daddy? Please, can I?'

'I can't take him, Dad,' Saf said, before Pete had time to answer. 'He runs all over the place. He won't stay with me, you know what he's like.'

Pete put out a hand and ruffled Stevie's hair. He wasn't in the mood for arguing with Saf. 'Maybe another time, eh, Stevie? Saf's getting to know her way around here now, so you can go with her soon, I promise.'

As Saf disappeared through the door, Pete called, 'You should pop in and see if Rhianna's home. I'm sure she'd love a trip to the park with you. Auntie Becky says she's beginning to think you don't like her any more!'

But Saf wasn't heading for the park. Not yet anyway. And she couldn't possibly invite Rhianna with her where she *was* going.

Saf had two things planned for that morning.

First, she was going to walk to the cemetery to visit Kevin's dad's grave.

Next, she was going to find Dixons.

Saf hadn't been to the cemetery since Kevin had taken her there to show her where his dad was buried. Partly she wanted to go to see whether he had been back and tidied the grave up. Not that she was really expecting that. That's why on her way out, she'd picked up an old pair of scissors from their garden shed, and put them in a carrier bag to take with her. If nothing else, she could trim the grass if it still hadn't been touched.

But there was another reason for setting off to the cemetery that morning. A very big and important reason.

The night before, Saf had asked her dad, 'Are we ever going home?'

Pete had frowned. 'What do you mean, Saf? We *are* home.'

'You *know* what I mean,' Saf persisted. 'Home. Our real home.'

'This is our real home now.'

'No! I want to go home. I want to be able to visit Mum's grave. I want to look after it.'

'Sweetheart,' Pete had sighed heavily. 'Mum's grave is being looked after. Really properly. Really carefully. I've organised all of that, you know I have. You don't have to worry. It's best that we don't go back. Really it is. It'll make it easier for you and Stevie if we concentrate on settling in here and making our new life.'

What you mean, Saf thought, is that it'll make it easier for you. You're the one who can't deal with it. You're the one who wants to pretend it never happened. As if Mum never existed.

At least, that's how it seemed to Saf. Her dad didn't care if she was happy or not.

So she'd decided. Another decision made all by herself. Something else no one would know about. If Kevin still wasn't looking after his dad's grave, Saf would do it. She'd make sure the grass was tidy, and she'd bring flowers. She'd do it for Kevin Alan Cole, Kevin-the-Dixon's dad, and she'd do it for her mum. If she couldn't care for the actual place where her mum was buried, she'd look after this place instead. It might make her feel better. As if she was doing something for her mum whether her dad wanted her to or not.

Walking up to the cemetery's big, rusty gates, Saf could hear the grinding rumble of a lawnmower. There was a man on a sit-on mower driving it backwards and forwards across the stretch of grass nearest to the entrance. This was the part that had been cut when Saf last came here. She wondered whether the man would carry on mowing a little further into the graveyard this time. Whether he noticed her or not, she couldn't be sure. If he did, he didn't call out 'hello' or glance her way.

Saf traipsed between the headstones to the far side of the cemetery. She found the spot easily enough.

Just as she had thought, it didn't look as if Kevin had been back here. If he had, he certainly hadn't done anything about neatening up the grave.

Saf did what she could. First she used the scissors to hack away at the grass. They were a bit blunt so she wasn't able to make a very smooth job of it. She took special care around the little wooden cross bearing Kevin's dad's name. Then she wandered around close by, picking up the bits and pieces of litter that had been dropped, or blown there by the wind. She tucked it all into the carrier bag with the scissors.

What Saf didn't have was any flowers, but she'd spotted some dandelions. They grew in clusters near the iron palings at the edge of the cemetery. Other people called dandelions 'weeds'. If you found them in your garden, you were supposed to dig them out. You had to get rid of them before their golden flower heads turned into fluffy puffballs of grey seeds. If the seeds were allowed to blow away on the breeze, they'd settle on the ground to grow new dandelion flowers; new dandelion flowers that nobody wanted. Saf could never understand why people didn't like them. She thought they were beautiful.

She picked a bunch with some leaves as well, then arranged them in a fan shape on the patch of scissor-cut grass.

Standing back to admire her handiwork, Saf couldn't help smiling.

'There, Kevin Alan Cole,' she murmured. Then, 'I love you, Mum.'

As she walked back through the cemetery gates, the lawnmower was standing just outside. The mowing man, however, was nowhere to be seen.

The next part of Saf's morning wasn't going to be so straightforward. She wanted to find Dixons, but she had no idea where they'd be.

Her first idea was to go to Rock Road and wait for them outside their den. But she might wait there all day and they'd never turn up. So perhaps the best place to start looking for them was in the park. They seemed to spend quite a lot of time there. The chances were she'd run into them sooner or later.

As it turned out, it was sooner. Saf hadn't even quite reached the park.

'It's the little girl!' Rick's voice rang out over the noise of a bus growling as it pulled away from its stop. 'Off to the park, then? I think the toddlers' area should be about right for you. Do you want us to show you where it is?'

Saf scowled at him. 'I'd be surprised if you could find anything with all that hair in your eyes,' she retorted.

'Oooh! Fighting talk, is it?' Rick glanced round smugly at the other two Dixons. Clyde was grinning, but Kevin's eyes were fixed on the pavement. 'What's the matter, Kev?' Rick went on. 'Don't you want me picking on your girlfriend?'

Kevin just shrugged and shoved his hands deeper into his pockets. 'She's not my girlfriend,' he grunted. He didn't even look at Saf. 'Why do you keep saying that?'

Rick and Clyde sniggered.

Saf stared at Kevin hard. 'Have you ever stood up for anyone, Kevin?'

He didn't answer.

'Anyway,' Saf said determinedly, 'who needs you? Who needs any of you? What I want is another time trial.'

There was a second's pause. Then Clyde and Rick burst out laughing. Saf's announcement even made Kevin look up.

Saf hadn't expected the laughter. She thought they'd shout, 'Forget it!' or, 'Not on your life!' but she didn't think they'd laugh.

Deep inside her, she felt a shiver. Only it wasn't fear. It was anger. How dare they? How dare they think they were so much better than she was? Clenching up her fists, she looked from one to the other. Right into their eyes.

'You think that's funny, you wait till I beat you,' she said. 'I don't want to be part of Dixons and I don't want your stupid den. I just want another time trial. And if you don't let me have one,' she added, tilting her chin up provokingly, 'it must be because you're scared of losing!'

That's when Dixons stopped laughing.

For a moment no one spoke. Kevin kept glancing nervously at the other two boys, but they didn't look at him.

'All right, then,' nodded Rick finally. 'What are we waiting for? Let's go and do it now.'

As usual, there was no one around at the end of Rock Road. No one to see them head down the side of the building site. The Dixons boys marched in front of Saf and climbed over the fence before her. On the other side, they didn't wait for her, just made straight for the fire escape. So Kevin didn't get the chance to see how easily Saf scaled the fence. She'd got very good at it because of all the times she'd been back there, practising on the stairs. Not that Dixons knew anything about that, of course.

They were just about to find out.

On the top floor, Saf was last to go again. It wasn't her choice. Rick told her she could go last. He went first. Clyde held the watch.

Thirty-eight seconds. Same as last time, Saf thought.

Next was Kevin … Thirty-eight seconds, too. He was quicker before.

Then Clyde, with Rick holding the watch … Thirty-seven seconds.

'Yes, yes!' he shouted. 'I knew I was going to win today!'

And suddenly, they were all looking at Saf again.

Her mouth was dry. Her heart thumped. What if it all went wrong? What if she couldn't beat any of them? It was just like the last time!

Except that it wasn't.

Because this time, Saf knew exactly what she was doing. This time, dry mouth or no dry mouth, shaky legs or no shaky legs, *she would beat them.*

'Go, little girl!' Rick leaned forward and screamed it right in her ear.

It made her jump and shoot forward before she was quite ready. She almost lost her balance and half slid down the first flight. Then she recovered – and she was off.

Fast.

Faster than Dixons ever thought she'd be.

Fast all the way down. She took barely a second to twist round at the bottom before launching herself back upwards again.

Fast enough to beat them.

As she leapt back onto the top landing, panting and hot, Rick was already shaking his head. 'That's not right. There's something wrong with this stupid watch, that's not right!'

'What does it say?' Clyde grabbed the watch. Then he shook his head, too. 'No, no way. That's impossible. It must need new batteries or something.'

'What is it?' Saf demanded breathlessly. 'What's my time?'

'I don't know, because the watch is wrong!' yelled Rick.

'Thirty-two seconds,' mumbled Kevin. He'd been looking at the watch display over Rick's shoulder. 'You did it in thirty-two seconds.'

Rick whirled around to face him. 'Shut up, Kev! She didn't do it in thirty-two seconds. No one could ever do it in thirty-two seconds! My watch is broken! Haven't you been listening to me?'

Kevin took a step backwards. 'Whatever.'

Saf pushed her fringe back and wiped her damp forehead with the palm of her hand. 'I beat you, then,' she said as matter-of-factly as she could manage, although the corners of her mouth were twitching with delight.

Clyde suddenly gave her a shove. Not hard, really, but nastily. His face twisted up nastily, too. 'You did *not* beat us!' he hissed. 'Don't you understand plain English? THE WATCH IS BROKEN!'

'Of course she doesn't understand plain English,' growled Rick. 'She's just a silly, pathetic, LITTLE GIRL!'

Saf stared at them, her teeth clenching together. This wasn't right. This wasn't how it was meant to go at all. She had beaten them! Why couldn't they just admit it?

She turned to Kevin. 'Say something, Kevin. You saw the time. Tell them I'm the winner! You know I am. Back me up! Why don't you say something?'

But Kevin never said a word. He wouldn't even look at her.

'You're the ones who're pathetic!'

Saf shouted at last. 'I beat you! *I'm* the winner! *Me*, not you! You're all just a bunch of losers and you always will be!'

She pushed through them to the top of the staircase and was gone.

Eleven

Saf ran off so quickly, she didn't hear what happened next.

She didn't see Rick round on Kevin almost instantly.

'This is all your fault!' Rick screeched. 'You should never have brought her here! This is our place. *Ours*! Dixons' Den, no one else's. You had no right to bring her. Why did you? Don't you get it, you've wrecked it now!'

'He's right, Kevin,' hissed Clyde. 'This was our secret and you've chucked it away. Like it doesn't even matter. Well, you know what?' He thrust his face close to Kevin's. 'Maybe it's time Dixons chucked *you* away.'

Kevin looked stunned. 'What?'

'What?' echoed Clyde, mocking the other boy's shocked expression.

'You heard him,' snarled Rick. At that moment, his voice grated with something that sounded like hatred. 'You're not one of us any more.'

Kevin's eyes flicked desperately from one boy to the other. 'That's stupid,' he gulped. 'I never meant ... Look, I'm sorry, all right? Saf's just a silly little kid, I know that. But I just thought, if she could come here sometimes instead of always having to go to the park, then those Topz wouldn't keep getting at her.'

Rick looked at him as if he couldn't understand what Kevin was talking about. 'Do you think we care, Kevin? We had a secret hideout and now, because of you, it's not a secret any more.' His mouth was pinched up furiously. 'I think it's time you left, don't you?'

'Left what? The den, you mean ... not the gang.'

'We don't have a "den" any more, Kevin,' growled Clyde. 'You made sure of that the minute you brought that girl here. You broke our rules. That means you can get out of Dixons.'

'No!' Kevin shook his head wildly. Determinedly. 'No, I'm not going. I said I was sorry. You can't *make* me leave.'

Clyde and Rick glanced at each other.

'Come on, Rick,' Clyde said. 'Let's get out of here. I don't know about you, but I can smell something *really* bad.'

Rick sniggered in response, darted one more scornful look at Kevin, then pushed him out of the way as he and Clyde ran off down the stairs.

All Kevin could do was stare helplessly after them.  The disbelief was stamped all over his face.

Then – 'Saf was right about one thing!' he yelled. 'You *are* losers!'

Neither Kevin nor Saf slept well that night.

The weather was hot and sticky. There wasn't a breath of wind. Even with her window wide open, Saf's room felt stifling. Airless.

'I think we might be in for a thunderstorm,' her dad had remarked at suppertime.

'But I don't like thunderstorms,' Stevie whined. 'Do we have to have one?'

Pete smiled. 'If there's one on the way,' he said, putting out a hand to squeeze Stevie's shoulder comfortingly, 'I'm afraid there's not a lot we can do to stop it.'

In the end, a storm didn't come to keep them all awake with its noise and sizzling lightning bursts. But Saf lay awake anyway.

She was stinging inside. She'd beaten Dixons. She'd run up and down those stairs so much faster than they ever had. And they'd still treated her as if she was a piece of rubbish. No better than the bits of dirty litter she'd picked up from around Kevin Alan Cole's grave.

'Talk to me if you need a friend.' That's what John had said to her a short while before, hadn't he? *'Best of all, talk to God.'*

At that moment, what Saf desperately did need was a friend. But she couldn't talk to John because it was the middle of the night. He was probably fast asleep. Even if he was awake like she was with the heat and the stuffiness, she could hardly go banging on his door now. She didn't believe John wanted to be her friend that much.

So what about God? Could she talk to Him as she lay in the darkness? Could she tell Him how all alone she felt? Just as she'd talked to Him about her mum?

Saf could feel the night's silence hanging in her bedroom. It seemed to cling to her as heavily as the muggy air.

'Please, God,' she found herself murmuring, *'I don't know how to feel better any more. Everything I do makes things worse and worse. I just want to be happy again and I don't think I ever will be …'*

Her voice trailed away into the blackness of her room.

That's all she said.

She hadn't spoken to God since that other night. The one just before her mum had died. Until that moment, she hadn't really known why.

As the last word floated away from her, Saf realised that she hadn't talked to God again because she didn't feel important enough. She could pray for her mum because her mum was the most amazing mum in the whole world. She was so worth praying for.

But however much Saf desperately needed to talk to God about her *own* feelings – however much she needed to ask Him to help *her* – she couldn't.

Saf felt like the least special person in the entire universe.

Kevin had never been so glad to see the morning. He'd lain awake all night, too, hot and uncomfortable.

One moment he was thinking that Clyde and Rick couldn't possibly have meant what they said. They wouldn't really kick him out of Dixons, would they? Then the next, he was muttering to himself furiously that he'd never rejoin the gang now, even if they begged him.

He sloped off out of the house early. But as he stood outside on the pavement, he suddenly realised he had nowhere to go. He couldn't head for the shopping centre or the park. He'd be more than likely to run into Dixons there. He didn't want to go to the building site either. Even though they'd said it wasn't their den any more, Kevin didn't think for one minute that they'd really stop going there.

That's when it came to him. He could walk to the cemetery.

This wasn't the first time since taking Saf there that Kevin had wondered about visiting his dad's grave. Saf had got him thinking about Kevin Alan Cole again; remembering things his sister had told him about his dad. He was even planning to ask his mum if she could dig out any old photos. She must still have some, at the back of a cupboard or tucked away in a drawer.

But he hadn't done anything about it yet because he was always doing something else. And it usually involved Dixons.

Kevin set off briskly. The sky was lead grey, but the weather was still uncomfortably hot. He was sweating before he'd reached the edge of the estate. He didn't want to slow his pace, though. Dixons could be anywhere.

As he reached the cemetery gates and began to weave his way through the headstones, it never occurred to him there would be anyone else around. After all, it was early, and this certainly wasn't one of the busier places in Holly Hill.

So when he spotted a figure in the distance, he froze.

Stopped stone still.

Not only was there someone in the cemetery with him, but they were actually sitting cross-legged on the grass beside his dad's grave.

Even before the figure on the ground looked up, Kevin knew exactly who it was.

Saf just about froze when she saw him, too. Just as she was the last person he was expecting to see, never in a million years did she think Kevin would show up here. He hadn't bothered in all this time. Why would he bother now?

Suddenly Kevin was striding towards her. Saf scrambled to her feet. He looked angry, she thought, but then she was angry, too.

'What is it with you, Saf or Saffron, whatever your name is?' he shouted. 'Everywhere I go lately, there you are! I'm sick of you turning up. You've got no business being anywhere, do you understand me? Especially not here!'

'I've got every business being here!' Saf yelled back. 'You weren't taking care of it, so now *I* am. It's got nothing to do with you. I'm doing it for your dad and my mum. So why don't you just go home?'

Kevin glanced down. He could hardly believe his eyes. 'Is this you?' he demanded. He stared at the roughly-cut grass and the fan of recently picked dandelions. 'Did you do this?'

'Of course I did. I care about making it nice, which is a lot more than you do.'

In an instant, Kevin's feet were flailing about, kicking the yellow flowers away and stamping all over them.

'What are you doing?' Saf gasped. 'Stop it! Why are you doing that?'

'Because you've ruined everything!' Kevin stood for a moment, breathing heavily. 'Thanks to you, I'm out of the den and out of Dixons. I've got *nothing* now!'

Saf frowned. 'What do you mean you're out of Dixons? What have they done?'

'They've kicked me out, haven't they? And it's all your fault!'

'What?' Saf could hardly take it in. Could Clyde and Rick really have banned Kevin from the gang just because she'd beaten them in a time trial? Would they honestly be that petty?

'Kevin – ' She went to take a step towards him, but he held up a hand to stop her.

'You stay away from me!' His voice rose to a shriek. 'Better still get out of here. In fact get out of Holly Hill! I never want to see you again! **NOT EVER!'**

As Saf began to run and stumble her way towards the cemetery gates, a drizzly rain was starting to fall, but she never felt it. Her mind was fixed on something else altogether.

She *would* get out of Holly Hill.

Not because Kevin wanted her to. What he wanted wasn't worth caring about.

No. Somehow or other, she was going to get herself home. Her real home. The only place where she could feel close to her mum again.

Right at that exact moment, Saf made up her mind to run away.

Twelve

Her dad was weeding in the front garden when Saf stormed through the gate.

'Saf? Saf, what's the matter now?'

She didn't answer and Pete thought perhaps now wasn't the time to go chasing after her. He didn't know how to deal with her moods these days. Her mum would have been good at that. Pete tended to leave her to herself and then try to talk to her when she'd calmed down.

Stevie, on the other hand, took no notice of Saf's 'grumps', as he called them. As she burst through the front door and raced straight upstairs to her bedroom, he was already running after her.

'Saf!' he yelled.

Saf answered him by slamming her bedroom door shut. But a closed door was never enough to keep Stevie out.

'Saf, why did you shut your door?' he said, pushing it open again. 'I want to talk to you.'

'Get out of my room, Stevie!' she snapped. 'I'm busy.'

'No, you're not,' he retorted. 'You're not doing anything.'

'Yes, I am!'

Saf pushed him out of the way so that she could get to her wardrobe to pull out a rucksack.

'What do you want that for?' Stevie asked.

'Go away, Stevie!'

'No! Why have you got your rucksack?'

'I told you to go *away*!'

Stevie clearly had no intention of going anywhere.

Next thing, Saf was yanking open drawers and flinging clothes onto her bed ready to pack.

'What are you doing now?' Stevie began again. 'You're making a mess. Daddy won't like it. You know he says we have to be tidy.'

'I don't care what Dad says!' she shouted. 'I just want you to leave me alone!'

Stevie was frowning now, but he didn't move.

Saf let out a cry of frustration. How could she pack to leave Holly Hill with her little brother standing right in front of her? She couldn't even think straight; couldn't make any sort of plan.

'Why don't you leave me alone?' she screeched finally. 'You *never* leave me alone!'

With that, she scooped everything up and stuffed it underneath her bed, along with the rucksack. She'd have to sort it out later. Stevie couldn't know what she was going to do. In any case, what she needed right at that moment was to be by herself. That was never going to happen as long as she was in the house.

Shoving past her little brother, she hurtled back down the stairs.

'Where are you going?' Stevie demanded.

'Out!'

Saf ran through the kitchen and out of the back door. Her dad was still in the front garden. She could avoid him going out the back way. She certainly didn't see why she should have to answer his questions as well.

What never occurred to her in a million years was that Stevie would follow her.

Stevie didn't run straight after her and catch her up. If he did that, he knew Saf would march him right back home again. But, he decided, if he followed along a little way behind, she'd never know he was there. Not till they were in the park anyway. Then she'd probably just play with him, because she was there and he was there, so she might as well. They could walk back together later.

But Saf wasn't going to the park. She wanted to be on her own. Completely on her own. As Kevin might still be at the cemetery, the only place she could think of was Dixons' Den. Hopefully, Clyde and Rick wouldn't already be there – they didn't seem to visit in the mornings. She'd discovered that when she'd been sneaking in to practise for her time trial.

At the end of Rock Road, Stevie hesitated. The streets around Holly Hill were very busy, but fortunately several drivers had stopped to let him across after Saf. Probably because he was so small. Stevie had waved 'thank you' to them, just as he'd seen his dad do. To start with, this whole expedition had felt like an adventure. A game. But he was beginning to feel nervous. He'd never been to the Dixons Estate before. He didn't have a clue where he was. All he was fairly sure of was that they were nowhere near the park.

In the distance, Stevie could see Saf heading for a building site at the end of the road. He couldn't lose sight of her, not now. If he did, he thought, he'd never find his way home. He could be lost here forever! So he ran forward a little way, then slowed again as Saf started to walk along the edge of the site.

Where *was* she going?

A few steps further, and he saw her climb up and over the fence, then march on round the side of the unfinished flats.

This was odd. *So odd.* But then a lot of the time, Stevie thought Saf *was* odd. So the fact that, here she was, doing something else peculiar perhaps wasn't such a surprise.

She was out of sight now. It'd be all right, though. All Stevie had to do was follow her over the fence.

Then he'd find her again. But he'd have to be quick.

Stevie stretched up his arms and stuck his fingers through the metal mesh. Then he tried to pull himself up, scrabbling with his toes to find a foothold. He'd just watched Saf get over. This must be how to do it. But all his feet seemed to do was flail around pointlessly. They kept slipping. He couldn't get enough grip to try to push himself upwards. By now, the fencing was cutting into his hands. In the end he had to let go, scrunching his sore fingers into his palms to try and stop them hurting.

After a moment, he tried again. This time it hurt even more and he still hadn't even begun the climb.

Suddenly Stevie was scared. He was stuck on one side of the fence. Saf was on the other. And he had no idea how to find his way home again. Tears began to sting the backs of his eyes. He lifted a thumb to his mouth and chewed on the stubby nail.

He was just about to shout Saf's name as loudly as he could, when he spotted it. A little further along the fence was a tiny gap. Two of the mesh panels were slightly crossed over each other at the top, making a small, triangular-shaped hole at the bottom. Stevie ran over to it. It was very tiny, but if he wriggled along on his tummy, he was sure he could get through. He stretched out on the ground. He put his head down and bit by bit, shoving with his shoulders and inching forwards, he pushed his way into the building site. The fencing dragged at his T-shirt and he scraped his elbow on a stone, but it didn't matter. In a moment, he'd managed to crawl through to the other side.

Stevie got to his feet. He was so pleased with himself, and so relieved that any minute now he'd find Saf, that he didn't even notice the mud smeared all down his front. All of a sudden, the adventure was fun again! Saf would be so surprised to see him that she wouldn't be cross. 'Oh, well,' she'd say. 'Now you're here, we may as well go to the park.'

He ran around the side of the flats, following Saf's route. Then he stopped. There was a door opening in the wall. Standing in front of it uncertainly, Stevie looked all around. There was no sign of his sister anywhere. She must have gone into the building. He took a couple of steps forward until he was just inside. Glancing towards the concrete staircase, he wondered what could be up there. The whole place looked grim and grey. It smelt funny, too. A mix of dust and mud and damp that seemed to catch in the back of his throat. Again it occurred to him to call out – but then he heard it.

The sound of running.

The drumming of trainers on the concrete steps.

Stevie caught his breath. It must be Saf, mustn't it? Of course it must … but … what if it wasn't?

The little boy jumped back just outside the door. He heard the feet land on the ground floor in a final spring, then twist and start to pelt back up again. Peeping round the corner, he just caught sight of Saf as she disappeared up onto the second flight.

An impish grin spread across Stevie's face. He had no idea why Saf was running back upstairs, but he knew she had to come down again. When she did, he'd give her such a fright!

Once more, Stevie hid just outside the door. He strained his ears; listening and listening. Would she run down straight away? How long would he have to wait?

No time at all. The footsteps had died away as Saf reached the top floor, but already they were getting closer again.

When Stevie was sure Saf must be almost at the bottom, he leapt through the doorway in full view.

'BOO!' he yelled at the top of his voice. Then he spluttered with laughter. At least, he thought he did.

Stevie saw Saf's eyes flash wide open in surprise.

He heard her scream. First with shock because he'd jumped out at her.

Next, because she was falling.

Then everything somehow stopped.

Losing her footing at the top of the final flight, Saf found herself diving headfirst down the steps. Stevie seemed to freeze. He couldn't have moved if he'd tried to. His feet were rooted to the spot.

Until Saf crashed heavily into him as she landed.

Then he was knocked flying.

Saf didn't move. It was as if the building was empty again. There was just the silence; the stillness; and the thick smell of dust and mud and damp.

At last she moaned quietly. She tried to move, but her neck hurt. Her head hurt. Her right arm was trapped underneath her and her wrist was throbbing horribly.

Pushing awkwardly with her other arm, Saf managed to sit up. She winced as she lifted her head. Then she looked round.

Stevie was lying by the fire escape door. His face was turned away from her.

'Stevie?'

Saf said his name again. Louder this time. Perhaps he hadn't heard her.

'Stevie?'

Slowly, painfully, she managed to drag herself towards him. 'Come on, Stevie, say something. You're not funny, you know.'

But Stevie didn't even murmur. As Saf leaned over him to see into his face, he looked for all the world as if he was fast asleep.

Except that, try as she might, **Saf couldn't wake him up.**

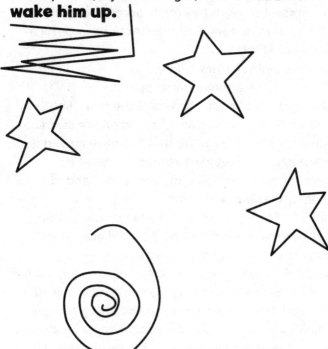

Thirteen

Pete groaned as he straightened up from the flowerbed he'd been weeding. Placing his hands low on his back, he stretched slightly. He ached from being bent over. 'Ow! Must be getting old!' he muttered to himself.

He glanced towards the house. How was Saf now? She'd flounced moodily through the garden a while earlier. Had she calmed down? Perhaps this was a good moment to go and have a chat. He could make himself a cup of coffee. He looked at the pile of weeds on the grass beside him, then back to the flowerbed he'd been working on. A satisfied smile spread across his face. He was doing a good job out here. It was definitely time for coffee.

At the front door, Pete slid off his boots. Then he stepped into the hallway calling, 'How's it going in here, troops? If anyone wants to do any weeding, you're welcome to lend a hand.'

No answer.

'Don't all shout at once.'

Again nothing. Silence.

Strange, Pete thought. The house was never this quiet.

He put his head round the lounge door before checking the kitchen. Then, 'Saf! Stevie!' he called, heading upstairs. 'Come on, you two, where are you hiding?'

But Saf and Stevie weren't anywhere in the house.

Pete stood in Saf's room, his hands on his hips. A deep frown began to dig itself into his forehead. As he turned, he caught sight of Saf's rucksack. It was sticking out from under her bed. There was something else there, too. Crouching down, he pulled out a scrunched up bundle of clothes. Dirty washing, perhaps ... No, these clothes were clean. He dropped them on the bed and went to check the drawers in the painted chest.

A couple of them were empty.

At the same moment, Pete spotted Saf's phone on the floor. He picked it up, his heart sinking even further. It must have fallen out of her pocket. She wouldn't have left it behind on purpose. Why would she?

Pete swallowed hard. Where were his kids? *Where were they?* He'd only been out in the front garden. Surely he'd have noticed if they'd left the house? In any case, they would have said something. How could his kids just not be here? And Saf knew better than to take Stevie out on her own ...

That was it! That had to be it! Saf must have taken Stevie to the park. Stevie had been on and on about wanting to go with her. They must have slipped out the back way. Why hadn't Saf told him what they were doing? All part of her moodiness, maybe. It made him angry. But at the same time, the thought that he'd find the two of them playing happily on the swings in the park helped him force down the panic in his stomach.

Pete walked quickly. Every moment he hoped he'd spot them; hoped he'd hear Stevie's shrill voice calling, 'Daddy!' Marching in through the park gates, he glanced over at the play equipment. It was busy. The early morning rain had dried up and there were lots of children running, climbing, sliding and swinging. But there was no sign of Saf or Stevie.

He strode closer, muttering over and over, 'Where are you? *Where are you?'*

There was a sudden whooping and cheering over in the skateboard park. Pete turned his head. Four boys were playing with a go-kart. They were from that Topz Gang, he was sure of it. He ran towards them.

'Excuse me!' he shouted. 'Excuse me, can I have a word, please?'

'That's Saf's dad, isn't it?' said John, looking round.

'I think it is,' nodded Paul, and he waved.

'Morning,' greeted Pete, trying not to sound as alarmed as he felt. 'I don't suppose any of you have seen Saf or Stevie?'

But of course they hadn't, because Saf and Stevie weren't in the park.

Pete's head drooped.

'Is everything all right?' John asked.

'I don't know,' Pete muttered. 'I'm not sure where Saf and Stevie are. I thought they were in the house, but ...' He paused for a moment. 'I was really hoping I'd find them here.'

'Where have you looked?' Danny asked.

'Just here, really,' Pete replied. 'Never mind, I'm sure they're somewhere around. I'll try down at the shopping centre.'

'We could try for you, if you like,' offered John. 'We're not doing anything.'

'That's right,' added Paul. 'Just messing with my go-kart. I keep crashing anyway.'

'Can't steer to save his life,' grinned Dave.

Pete managed a half-hearted smile. 'If you really don't mind, that'd be great.'

'Of course we don't mind,' said John. 'I like Saf a lot.'

Pete decided to keep looking in the park. He still felt it was the most likely place the two of them would be.

Dave and Danny headed for the shopping centre. John and Paul said they'd drop the go-kart off at Paul's house, then start walking around the streets where Saf and Stevie lived. Perhaps they'd gone exploring together and got lost. Saf might not know her way about that well yet.

John and Paul had only just left the park when they spotted Kevin. He was sauntering past the newsagents, head down, hands in pockets, and kicking a small stone along in front of him. The other two Dixons were nowhere to be seen.

John gave Paul a nudge. 'Do you think he might know where Saf and Stevie are?'

Paul shrugged. Neither of them especially wanted to go up to Kevin and ask him, but he and Saf did hang about together sometimes. He might have some idea.

'You could ask, I suppose,' Paul answered reluctantly.

'Stay here a minute,' said John.

He crossed the road and ran towards the newsagents. 'Kevin!'

Kevin looked up, startled. Whoever he thought it might be calling to him, the last person he expected to see was John. As he'd said to Saf, Topz and Dixons didn't mix, and a Topz had never been known to chase after a Dixon in the street before.

'What do *you* want?' Kevin grunted.

'I was just wondering if you'd seen Saf,' John began awkwardly. 'I mean, you probably haven't. But I know you sometimes do ... Only her dad was looking for her. She's missing. Well, not "missing" exactly, but he can't find her or her little brother. So, if you've got any idea where they might have gone ... well, it might help find them, that's all.'

Kevin was scowling all over his face. 'How should I know where she is?' he muttered. 'And why should I care anyway? She's a creep. Her brother's probably a creep, too.'

'I just thought –'

'Well, stop thinking, Topz boy! I don't know where they are, all right?' Then he rammed his shoulder hard into John's as he pushed him out of the way.

John watched him slope off, then glanced over the road at Paul and shook his head. No clue from Kevin.

However, the irritating thing for Kevin was that he *did* have a clue. As he walked along, he tried to put Saf out of his mind. He didn't care if she was missing or not. Why should he? She'd wrecked his life. He'd lost his two best friends because of her.

Still, he couldn't help wondering where she'd gone after their meeting in the cemetery that morning. He'd shouted at her. He'd been really nasty. I mean, so what, she deserved it, he thought to himself – but that voice inside his head just wouldn't stop nagging at him …
Supposing she's gone back to Dixons' Den?

Kevin stopped still. No, she'd be mad to have done that. If Clyde and Rick caught her there, he didn't like to think what they'd do. Anyway, surely she wouldn't have taken her little brother there. That would be stupid, and Saf might be a lot of things, but stupid wasn't one of them.

Shoving his hands deeper in his pockets, Kevin gave the stone one last kick. He watched it scutter across the pavement and into the gutter. Then he carried on walking.

Saf could have been all alone on another planet.

The rest of the world seemed millions of miles away. There was just stillness. No one to help her. The only sound was her own whispers.

She knelt on the mucky, concrete floor, stroking Stevie's hair. Every now and then he opened his eyes and looked at her, but he didn't say a word.

'Come on, Stevie,' Saf kept repeating softly, over and over. 'You'll be all right. You've just got to get up. We need to go home. Dad'll be wondering where we are. Stevie, please try and get up. Please …'

The other whispers were a prayer.

I know You're there, God. I don't talk to You very much, but I can always feel You. You're looking at me now. You're looking at Stevie. This is all my fault. Stevie's hurt because of me. I'm sorry. I'm sorry I keep doing the wrong thing. I don't know why I do. I just miss Mum so much. And it's really scary but most of the time, I can't even remember what I used to be like before she died. I can't remember what it felt like to be happy; what it was like not being angry all the time.

Anyway, that's just me isn't it, God, so it doesn't matter. But Stevie matters. You know he matters, don't You? Then please help us get home. I just want us to be able to get home. I want my dad. Please, God, please hear me. Please hear me for Stevie. **Please** …

A sound outside ruffled the stillness. Saf looked up. Kevin was standing in the doorway.

Fourteen

For a moment, neither of them spoke.
Then Kevin stepped inside, eyeing the little boy on the floor uneasily.

'What's happened?'

'It's my brother.' Saf swallowed. She could feel tears she didn't want. 'I didn't know he was here. I was running on the stairs and I fell and … Stevie was in the way. I knocked into him. I didn't mean to, I didn't see him. He jumped out of nowhere … Have you got your phone on you?'

Kevin crouched down to peer at Stevie, eyes wide, staring.

'He must have hit his head,' Saf gulped. 'He's awake

now but he won't move. I keep asking him to get up. He can hear me. He hasn't said anything, not a word, but I know he can hear me. He just won't stand up.'

'What was he doing here?' Kevin said at last. 'No one's supposed to come here. No one's supposed to know about this place. How could you have let him come here?'

'I don't know,' Saf mumbled. 'I didn't tell him where I was going. He must have followed me. Please, Kevin, can I borrow your phone?'

'I haven't got one, I broke it. Followed you?' Kevin went on, his voice rising in disbelief. 'You let him *follow you* here?'

'I never thought! He's never done it before. Why would I think about that?'

Kevin started shaking his head. 'Stupid, *stupid* girl! You're nothing but trouble, do you know that? I should never have brought you here. I wish I'd never even met you!'

'What's wrong with you?' Saf spluttered. Her fear suddenly burst into anger. 'Can't you see Stevie's in trouble! This isn't about you or me, Kevin; it's about Stevie. He's hurt. He's really hurt! I've got to stay with him, I can't leave him here on his own. That means you're going to have to go for help. Please! And *quickly!*'

'Go for help?' Kevin almost looked as if he might start laughing. 'How can I go for help? People would find out we've been in here. Don't you get it? *We're not supposed to be here.* We'll be in so much trouble if anyone knows.'

'I don't care! I need you to help Stevie. You've got to get over to Holly Hill and fetch my dad.'

'He's already out looking for you.'

'What?'

'That's why I came. He's looking for you with that Topz Gang. I just had a feeling you'd be here.'

Just at that moment, Stevie moaned. Quietly. Saf reached out and took his hand. He squeezed her fingers gently. 'It's all right, Stevie,' she murmured. 'It'll all be fine. Kevin's going to get Dad and then we'll be home in no time.' She looked at Kevin pointedly. 'We will be fine, won't we, Kevin?'

Slowly, Kevin stood up. Stevie's face was pale-white. It was the whitest face Kevin had ever seen. What could he do? How could he just leave a little boy like that? Lying there like a frightened animal? But how could he tell anyone where he was either?

Backing away, Kevin's gaze shifted to Saf.

Then he spun round and disappeared through the doorway.

'Hurry!' Saf blinked into the space where he'd been. The moment he was gone, the stillness seemed to flood back like a wave. She didn't like it. It made her feel lost. Lost in empty space with Stevie.

And it was her fault.

There was another squeeze on her fingers. She half-smiled down into the whiteness of Stevie's face. 'Won't be long now, Stevie,' she said. 'I bet you won't ever follow me again after this, will you? ... I'm so sorry. I never meant for you to get hurt. I'm so, so sorry. Dad'll be here soon, I promise.'

Saf knew she shouldn't really promise because she didn't really know. Kevin was clearly so scared to tell anyone about Dixons' Den that he might just go straight home. In any case, he hated her now. Even if he saw her dad or Topz, he might not say a word. She'd only know if they came.

The stillness of the unfinished building was like a weight, pressing in on her. The stillness and the silence.

'Tell you what, Stevie, I'm going to keep talking,' Saf began again. 'I feel better if I can hear someone talking. Even if it's only me. You can say something, too, if you want … if you can … I'd like that. That's weird, isn't it? Normally I want you to be quiet. But there's *a bit* quiet and there's *lots too* quiet, and at the moment this is all *lots too* quiet …

'Anyway, I've been meaning to ask you – do you ever talk to God, Stevie? Because you could talk to Him right now if you wanted to. He's here, you see. Remember what Mum used to say when she was ill? "You'll never be on your own. God will always be with you." Well, He is here with us, because I've been talking to Him. I've been asking Him to help you. Shall I speak to Him again? For both of us? I've got loads to say and I'm sure He won't mind if you're listening. I don't mind if you're

listening either. So that's what I'll do now, all right? I'll have a chat to God while we're waiting for Kevin to bring Dad.'

Saf leaned forward and brushed a wisp of blond hair out of Stevie's eye.

'I always wanted blond hair, Stevie,' she sighed. 'Trust you to end up with it and not me.' She fingered the flimsy curl thoughtfully.

I wonder why You gave Stevie blond hair and not me, God? Mum said her hair used to be blond when she was young, but as she grew up, it got darker. I was just born with the darker stuff right away. Dark and straight. It goes a bit wavy sometimes – in the rain. Not when it's heavy, but in that mizzly, damp sort that gets under umbrellas and inside hoods. It's OK, though. I mean, it's my hair and I think it suits me all right most of the time. I'd just quite like to have been blond.

There are lots of things I'd quite like, God. More important things than the colour of my hair. There's today, for instance. I'd like today to start all over again. I've been thinking about it. I'd like to have woken up this morning and not gone out. I'd like to have not even thought about visiting the cemetery. Then I wouldn't have seen Kevin, and I wouldn't have got cross, and I wouldn't have come here. And if I hadn't come here, then neither would Stevie. So, what I'd really like is to have seen Dad working in the garden this morning and stayed at home and helped him.

I'd like to go back further than this morning, too. Back to before we came here. Back to before Mum died.

I was happy then. I knew what it felt like to be happy all the time. I had bad moods and sad days but that was just on the surface. Feelings that were here one minute, gone the next. Inside, I was always happy. And I know I can't have Mum back – I know that's impossible – but I'd like to go back to before I was angry all the time. Since I've been angry, I've done everything wrong. I've been so unhelpful to Dad. 'Be good for your dad,' Mum said, and I haven't been. I've been horrible. I didn't want to move here and I've blamed it all on him. And I suppose he was only trying to do what he thought was best. Best for me, best for Stevie.

I've just been feeling so unimportant, so un-special. As if what I wanted didn't count for anything. And I thought, if I don't matter at all to my dad, how am I going to matter to You, God? Why would You listen to me talking about me? So I didn't talk to You at all. I thought, I'll just work it all out for myself. I'll find ways of making myself feel better.

And now look at the mess I've made. What's Dad going to say when he sees Stevie like this? Lying on a dirty concrete floor. Stevie never stops talking and he hasn't said a word. Not one single word. We shouldn't even be here. What's Dad going to think of me when he knows I've been sneaking off and going to places he didn't know about? He'll be so disappointed in me when he finds out.

So that's why I want to go back, God. I want to go back and make everything all right again. I want You to make me all right again. Not angry. Not sad. Not doing things

I shouldn't be doing. Is it too late? You see, I'm sorry, I'm really so sorry. For everything. I want to start all over again. I want to be free, God. I don't want to be this angry person. I don't like it. I've just got so used to feeling this way, I don't know how to stop. But You'll help me, won't You? I know I'm not special like Mum was, but please could You still help me? I won't be able to do it on my own.

Something moved. Quickly. Lightly. Saf caught sight of it out of the corner of her eye. A small, brown bird had flown in through the doorway and landed just inside the building. It looked so tiny; so delicate on the concrete floor. Almost as if it had been blown there by the wind.

Saf stopped speaking and froze. She even held her breath. *Don't fly away,* she thought, keeping as still as she could. *You've come from somewhere out there. Where I've got to get back to with Stevie. Please stay. Don't fly away.*

She watched the bird as it hopped about in the dust, tilting its head this way and that. Exploring. Curious. It didn't seem to notice her or Stevie. Or if it did, it obviously wasn't bothered that they were there.

Have you been here before? Saf wondered. *Perhaps you've seen me running on the stairs.*

Out of the corner of Saf's other eye, she was suddenly aware of something else moving. She turned her head sharply.

The bird didn't fly away. Now Stevie was watching it, too. He'd propped himself up on one elbow to see better.

With a thin smile on his pale-white face, he said softly, 'Sparrow.'

Fifteen

Saf sat on the grass.

It was another hot day. Not uncomfortable, sticky hot under a heavy, grey sky, but warm and comforting like a cuddle. No clouds overhead. Just clear, gleaming blue, flooded with brilliant sunlight. Leaf shadows flickered under the trees. Playful. Dancing. On a high branch a blackbird perched, singing its heart out.

It was beautiful, Saf thought. All of it so beautiful.

And perfect. Just as it should be.

'Do you mind if I stay here on my own for a bit?' Saf had asked her dad.

'Of course, I don't,' Pete smiled. 'We'll go for a walk in the woods. Be back in a little while.'

'Yeah!' Stevie cheered. 'Can we look for conkers?'

'Might be a tiny bit early for conkers, yet,' Pete replied, 'but we'll see what else we can find, eh?'

Saf watched them wander away down the path and out through the arched wooden gateway.

And then she was alone. Listening to the blackbird's piping song. Enjoying the warmth of the sun. Gazing at the flowers they'd brought with them for her mum's grave. They were sunflowers. Saf had clustered them together in a bright yellow pot in front of the headstone. Saf's mum had loved sunflowers; their round, deep brown faces thickly fringed with a mass of golden petals. She'd loved the taste of the seeds, too, all crunchy and nutty.

'I know why hamsters always look so happy,' she said once. 'They get to snack on sunflower seeds whenever they want.'

Above the flowers, the inscription on the headstone stood out. Saf had chosen the words. 'They're the only ones that are right,' she'd told her dad.

They're still the only ones that are right, she thought, reading them again now.

BEST MUM IN THE WHOLE WORLD EVER

It's odd being back here, God. So odd but so wonderful. I never thought it would happen. I never thought I'd see any of this again. It seems as if I've been away forever, but it's only been a few weeks. And they haven't been good weeks, have they? I've done some bad things. But I have made some good friends.

I thought Kevin was my friend to start with. Only then

somehow that, when it mattered, he wouldn't let me down. He couldn't, could he? Not with Stevie lying there in trouble. And he didn't let me down either. He went looking for my dad.

I'm so pleased it was John he found first. I'm so glad John sat and talked to me while we waited there for my dad and the ambulance to come. That was You, wasn't it, God? You sent him. John said he'd been praying for just the right words and every single thing he said while we were huddled up in that empty, grey building was exactly right. Exactly what I needed to hear.

John said that bad things happen, but through them all, we should never stop trusting You and talking to You. And we must never think that we're not important or special to You because it's not true. You love us more than we can even begin to imagine.

I told John I didn't feel special at all. I said, 'And even if I was special to God once, how can I be special to Him now after I've been so horrible? After Stevie got hurt because of me?'

John said that as soon as I tell You I'm sorry, God, You forgive me. Just like that. I said, 'But how do you know? I bet you've never done anything really wrong in your whole life.' John laughed at that, didn't he? He said, 'Everyone does wrong things, Saf. We say wrong things; think wrong things; do wrong things. We try hard not to and we can ask God to help us, but in the end none of us is perfect. There's only ever been one perfect man and that's Jesus.'

Then John told me something else. He said, 'The reason I was so worried about you getting mixed up with Dixons is because I got mixed up with them once. Me – one of the Topz Gang. They wanted me to steal something and I did. I knew it was wrong, but I did it anyway. And I ended up feeling just like you. I thought, how will God ever forgive me? How will He ever feel the same about me now that I've done that? How will I even be able to forgive myself? But the minute I said sorry, God **did** forgive me. And the minute you say sorry, Saf, He'll forgive you, too. And if God, who's so huge and great and amazing and powerful, can forgive us, then don't you think we should forgive **ourselves**? Otherwise it's like being ungrateful for His forgiveness. So just say sorry, then believe that you're forgiven and be free. It's that simple – because that's what the Bible says.'

But, it wasn't just You I needed to say sorry to, was it, God? There was the Topz Gang. They'd all tried to be so kind and friendly and I'd just turned my nose up at them. And there was Rhianna. Poor Rhianna. She was so excited we were moving to Holly Hill, and I acted like I didn't care. Like I didn't even want to know her. It's going to be all right now. She says we can start all over again. Her, me, Topz. Just as if the last few weeks never happened. And that's what I wanted, isn't it, God? To be able to start again. That's what I talked to You about. Beginning with a clean sheet, Dad calls it.

Oh, my dad! I tried to say sorry to him, God, but he said no. He said if anyone should say sorry it was him. He said, 'I didn't really understand what losing your mum was like for you. I only knew what it was like for me. I thought if we moved away, had a completely new life, that would be better. Less painful in the end. I didn't realise how hard that would be for you, Saf. I didn't listen to you and I'm sorry. It's my fault you've been so angry, not yours. It's my fault you started keeping secrets from me. It's my fault Stevie ended up in hospital with a banged head.' He was nearly crying, my dad was. 'But I'm going to sort all of this out,' he said. 'We'll go back and visit Mum's grave. Not just once but when you feel you need to. As often as we can, we'll go back all together.' 'And can we take flowers?' I asked him. 'Of course, we can take flowers,' he smiled. Then he gave me a hug. Partly because he wanted to give me a cuddle, but partly I think he was trying to hide his tears. I'd already seen them, though.

And what about Kevin, God? He doesn't know You. He doesn't talk to You. He doesn't understand that You're just waiting for him to turn around and run into Your arms, so that You can hug him just like my dad hugged me. He's an angry boy, isn't he? He needs You, he just hasn't realised it yet.

When Kevin came back to the building site with John, he was going to run straight off again. He didn't want to be caught there when the ambulance came. But in the end he stayed because I asked him to. I told him I wouldn't give him away. I told him I'd never say Dixons used the site as their den. I don't know if he believed me then, but he believes me now. Of course, he's never been back there. It'd be too risky. And he warned Rick and Clyde not to go back either. He didn't have to do that, did he? He could have just let them get in trouble.

After all, they weren't very nice to him.

Anyway, because of that I suppose, they must have made up and now he's back in Dixons. That's probably not a good thing, but maybe one day he'll work that out for himself. Maybe every now and again, God, You could drop it into his head that he doesn't need Dixons. What he needs is a brand-new life. He won't talk to You at the moment, I know that. But that doesn't mean I can't talk to You about him.

And I have been talking to You about him, haven't I, God? Kevin didn't sit with John and me and Stevie while we were waiting for the ambulance. He stood over by the door with his hands in his pockets. He nearly always has his hands in his pockets. But he heard every word John said to me. All about being special to You and being forgiven when we say sorry. I know he was feeling guilty about Stevie. I could see it all over his face. If he'd never taken me to Rock Road and those flats at the end, Stevie wouldn't be needing an ambulance – that's what he was thinking. And as he listened to John, I was fairly sure he wanted Your forgiveness, too. I definitely wanted him to know he had mine.

That's why, when we heard all the footsteps coming round the side of the building – the ambulance men and my dad and Paul and Dave and Danny – I called over to him. 'It's all right, Kevin. I know you think this is your fault, but it's not. Whatever you think you've done to us … I forgive you.' That's what You want to say to Him, too, isn't it, God? I forgive you.

Kevin ran off just after that and I didn't see him for a while. Not even in the park when I went with Stevie and Rhianna to meet up with Topz and have a go on Paul's go-kart. So when Dad said we were coming up here this weekend, I had to go looking for him. Dad said it was all right.

I found him at the shopping centre. He was on his own which was good. I don't think I could have asked with Rick and Clyde there. I'm not even sure why I wanted to ask him at all. I just did.

'We're going back to my old home,' I told him. 'For a visit. We're going to put flowers on my mum's grave and I was wondering … if you'd like to come with us. You showed me where your dad's buried. That was special. At least, it was to me. Now I'd like to share this with you.'

Of course I didn't expect him to say yes. I'm not sure what I expected him to say. But the important thing was that I'd asked. That would show him, more than anything, that I was his friend and I really did forgive him. Then maybe he could stop blaming himself.

Thank You, dear God, that You forgive me. Thank You that I'm here right now. Thank You for my mum. Thank You that I'm part of two families – my own and Yours. Thank You for letting me go back and start again. Thank You for answering all these prayers of mine.

There were other voices now; drifting through the arched gateway and up the path to where Saf was sitting.

'We can come back soon, though, can't we?' Stevie was saying eagerly. 'In time to collect the conkers when they're ready.'

'Of course we can,' replied Pete. 'But I'm sure there must be conkers somewhere in Holly Hill.'

'There are,' said a third voice. 'There's a tree down the end of the park.'

'You see, Stevie?' smiled Pete.
'Conkers are everywhere.'

'Yeah! Conkers are everywhere!' Stevie cried.

The older boy behind him couldn't help grinning as he stuffed his hands deep into his pockets. What would Clyde and Rick say, he wondered, if they saw him out collecting conkers with a six-year-old?

Right at that moment, he didn't care.

Kevin was having one of the best days of his life.

NATIONAL DISTRIBUTORS

UK: (and countries not listed below)

CWR, Waverley Abbey House, Waverley Lane, Farnham, Surrey GU9 8EP.

Tel: (01252) 784700 Outside UK (44) 1252 784700 Email: mail@cwr.org.uk

AUSTRALIA: KI Entertainment, Unit 21 317-321 Woodpark Road, Smithfield, New South Wales 2164.

Tel: 1 800 850 777 Fax: 02 9604 3699 Email: sales@kientertainment.com.au

CANADA: David C Cook Distribution Canada, PO Box 98, 55 Woodslee Avenue, Paris, Ontario N3L 3E5.

Tel: 1800 263 2664 Email: sandi.swanson@davidccook.ca

GHANA: Challenge Enterprises of Ghana, PO Box 5723, Accra.

Tel: (021) 222437/223249 Fax: (021) 226227 Email: ceg@africaonline.com.gh

HONG KONG: Cross Communications Ltd, 1/F, 562A Nathan Road, Kowloon.

Tel: 2780 1188 Fax: 2770 6229 Email: cross@crosshk.com

INDIA: Crystal Communications, 10-3-18/4/1, East Marredpalli, Secunderabad – 500026, Andhra Pradesh.

Tel/Fax: (040) 27737145 Email: crystal_edwj@rediffmail.com

KENYA: Keswick Books and Gifts Ltd, PO Box 10242-00400, Nairobi.

Tel: (020) 2226047/312639 Email: sales.keswick@africaonline.co.ke

MALAYSIA: Canaanland, No. 25 Jalan PJU 1A/41B, NZX Commercial Centre, Ara Jaya, 47301 Petaling Jaya, Selangor.

Tel: (03) 7885 0540/1/2 Fax: (03) 7885 0545 Email: info@canaanland.com.my

Salvation Publishing & Distribution Sdn Bhd, 23 Jalan SS 2/64, 47300 Petaling Jaya, Selangor.

Tel: (03) 78766411/78766797 Fax: (03) 78757066/78756360 Email: info@salvationbook-centre.com

NEW ZEALAND: KI Entertainment, Unit 21 317-321 Woodpark Road, Smithfield, New South Wales 2164, Australia.

Tel: 0 800 850 777 Fax: +612 9604 3699 Email: sales@kientertainment.com.au

NIGERIA: FBFM, Helen Baugh House, 96 St Finbarr's College Road, Akoka, Lagos.

Tel: (01) 7747429/4700218/825775/827264 Email: fbfm_1@yahoo.com

PHILIPPINES: OMF Literature Inc, 776 Boni Avenue, Mandaluyong City.

Tel: (02) 531 2183 Fax: (02) 531 1960 Email: gloadlaon@omflit.com

SINGAPORE: Alby Commercial Enterprises Pte Ltd, 95 Kallang Avenue #04-00, AIS Industrial Building, 339420.

Tel: (65) 629 27238 Fax: (65) 629 27235 Email: marketing@alby.com.sg

SOUTH AFRICA: Struik Christian Books, 80 MacKenzie Street, PO Box 1144, Cape Town 8000.

Tel: (021) 462 4360 Fax: (021) 461 3612 Email: info@struikchristianmedia.co.za

SRI LANKA: Christombu Publications(Pvt)Ltd, Bartleet House, 65 Braybrooke Place, Colombo 2.

Tel: (9411) 2421073/2447665 Email: dhanad@bartleet.com

USA: David C Cook Distribution Canada, PO Box 98, 55 Woodslee Avenue, Paris, Ontario N3L 3E5, Canada.

Tel: 1800 263 2664 Email: sandi.swanson@davidccook.ca

CWR is a Registered Charity – Number 294387

CWR is a Limited Company registered in England – Registration Number 1990308

Topz is a colourful daily devotional for 7- to 11-year-olds.

In each issue the Topz Gang teach children biblical truths through word games, puzzles, riddles, cartoons, competitions, simple prayers and daily Bible readings.

Available as an annual subscription
£15.50 (6 bimonthly issues includes p&p)
or as single issues **£2.85**.

Go to **www.cwr.org.uk/store**,
call 01252 784700 or visit a Christian bookshop.

Prices correct at time of printing.

You'll also love
Topz Secret Diaries

Alexa Tewkesbury's *Topz Secret Diaries* hit the
balance between humour and insightful truth
as they bring well-loved Topz characters to life.

Benny's Barmy Bits
ISBN: 978-1-85345-431-8

Danny's Daring Days
ISBN: 978-1-85345-502-5

Dave's Dizzy Doodles
ISBN: 978-1-85345-552-0

**Gruff & Saucy's
Topzy-Turvy Tales**
ISBN: 978-1-85345-553-7

John's Jam-Packed Jottings
ISBN: 978-1-85345-503-2

Josie's Jazzy Journal
ISBN: 978-1-85345-457-8

Paul's Potty Pages
ISBN: 978-1-85345-456-1

Sarah's Secret Scribblings
ISBN: 978-1-85345-432-5

Go to **www.cwr.org.uk/store**,
call 01252784700 or visit a Christian bookshop.

Boys Only and Just for Girls

These special editions of *Topz Secret Diaries* will help you discover things about yourself and God with questions and quizzes, engaging puzzles, word searches, doodles, lists to write and more.

Topz Secret Diaries: Boys Only
ISBN: 978-1-85345-596-4

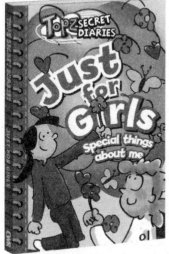

Topz Secret Diaries: Just for Girls
ISBN: 978-1-85345-597-1

126-page paperbacks, 129x197mm

Go to www.cwr.org.uk/store,
call 01252 784700 or visit a Christian bookshop.